Grave Circle

An Ivory Tower Mystery

Grave Circle

AN IVORY TOWER MYSTERY

DAVID D. NOLTA

QUALITY WORDS IN PRINT

Grave Circle
An Ivory Tower Mystery

Published by Quality Words In Print, LLC
P. O. Box 2704, Costa Mesa, California 92628–2704
www.qwipbooks.com

Interior Design & Typesetting by Desktop Miracles, Inc., Stowe, VT

LCCN: 2002094916

First Edition

**Publisher's Cataloging-in-Publication
*(Provided by Quality Books, Inc.)***

Nolta, David Derbin.
    Grave circle : a mystery / by David D. Nolta.
        p.   cm. – (An ivory tower mystery ; 1)
    ISBN 0–9713160–2–3

        1. Murder—Fiction.   2. College teachers—Fiction.
    3. Small colleges—Fiction.   4. Mystery Fiction.   I. Title.

PS3614.O65G73   2003   813'.6
                                                    QBI33–768

Printed in the United States of America

*This book is dedicated to
my mother and my father
(no mystery there)*

ACKNOWLEDGEMENTS

Over the years, I have been fortunate to know a number of people who have inspired, encouraged and assisted me in my literary endeavors. Aside from the members of my immediate family, the most notable of these kind accomplices are: Lorene Erickson, Pamela Erbe, James Magruder, Brighde Mullins, Sheila O'Connell, Tanya Cromey and Jon and Holly Gruber. When I succeed in my writing, it is for and because of them. When I do not, they are the reason I continue to try.

I

Antigone Musing might, at this moment, have been a painted illustration of the pensive state suggested by her name. She sat with uncharacteristic languor in the comfortably cushioned bay window of the 1920's Cape Cod which was the most attractive of the perquisites she enjoyed as a full-time faculty member at Clare College. Uncharacteristic, because idleness and ease were utterly foreign to her nature.

Antigone—or Tig, as she was known to her family and her rather few good friends—preferred always to be doing something. Not only did she have the proverbial restless curiosity of the scientist and the inexhaustible energy of the teacher, to both of which titles she had claim, but there was also something more, something very personal and no doubt subconscious which, even on those infrequent occasions when she could be persuaded to stand still for a photograph, rendered her appealingly vital and dynamic and as though in the act of discovery (a form, after all, of departure), or even escape. So this morning's complete resignation to a static, traceable outline against the late October, Massachusetts sky could only indicate one thing. She was soon to have a visitor.

No matter what you, the reader, may have been told, all academics, even those less serious or committed than our heroine—for I can tell you at the outset that she is our heroine—are always thrown into a state of upheaval by a visit of any kind. There are so many myths about the gracious manners and the time-tested behavioral practices prevailing in the ivory tower that for a majority of intelligent outsiders the world of academia has come to be seen as the last fortress of civilized society and, as such, a sacred model for all social interactions, a place like the palace in Urbino where Castiglione's whispers, though dwindling, can still be heard. The fact remains, however, that most faculty members who make up the ruling bodies of the American college campus have an aversion to actual physical meetings with their fellow human beings, repress or defy the feeling though they

might. And when, moreover, they are forced to con-
gregate, as regularly they must, they become the intellectual equivalents of cows competing at a country
fair, their movements marked by awkwardness, by
strange prides and even stranger premonitions.

Antigone was an exception to this rule, at least to
the extent that she was not a victim to the bumbling
and huffing displayed by her peers under the threat of
being in company. And this was only one of many reasons that she was marveled at and respected by her
students and colleagues alike. Nevertheless, there was,
indeed, a visit on her immediate horizon, and it was
the prospect of this visit which caused the alteration
of her manner, an alteration such as one might
observe in a clock which, after running fast for as long
as one can remember, suddenly winds down to a stop.
But, of course, her outward calm was inversely pro-
portionate to the busy state of her mind. Her dark
eyes swept slowly and inquiringly over the landscape
presented by the large tripartite window. She studied
each element of the scene as though she was seeing it
for the first time, and that was perhaps close to the
truth, for although she had been living in the cottage
for two years, it was not, as we have said, her habit to
lounge about, looking through windows. Now, to each
natural or architectural feature, she silently appended
a personal observation. To her left, the Mohawk trail,

pre-dating the august college as well as the small English settlement from which it grew, disappeared
upward into a hillside range of fir and oak trees, and
as it did, Antigone considered, with tacit facetious-
ness, the course her own life was taking, the future
direction of which was also rather obscure. Passing on
to the high brick clock tower, which constituted the
centerpiece of her view as it did of the college campus,
she was encouraged to remember that she had less
than half an hour before her visitor would arrive. And
finally, occupying the greater part of the fore- and
middle grounds sloping in both directions and beyond
her sight, was the lower range of stately, Gothic
revival and colonial structures which together composed the beautiful, widely-familiar panorama of
Clare College, the afternoon sunlight distinguishing
its favorite details, here sharpening the winged outline of a stone gargoyle, there setting ablaze the reflec-
tive surface of a fanlight or mullioned oriel.

And to this view of the college itself, spread out
before her like a timeless city in a dream or a devil's
bribe, Antigone brought innumerable thoughts, not
least among them the notion—a realization that came
and went, that never stayed long enough to fill her
with despair, but that never left her in peace altogether, that seemed in short to suggest without ever
forcing itself as a conclusion—that in this life she had

chosen, she would always feel, on the deepest and most secret level, alone. It may or may not strike the reader as surprising that, of all moments, this particular recurrent idea of her solitude struck the slim, attractive young woman, simply, even plainly but somehow perfectly, dressed, now, when she was about to play the host. But surely there are many who can identify with the feeling of solitude that is heightened by the presence, impending or already under way, of family. For it was her brother Hi—"Hi" being the shortest possible abbreviation of his real name, Hiawatha, used only by intimates of the family and, like her own name, a carefully guarded secret of their shared childhood—who was coming to stay with her, whose imminent arrival had appreciably relaxed her body as it animated both her spirit and her mind.

There was no one in the world closer to Antigone than her brother, Hiawatha. In fact, this closeness was often the subject of comments originating with their father, Mr. Michael Musing, who, since his own graduation from Yale College thirty-nine years ago, had been a respected teacher of literature at the best private high school in Boston, and his wife, Elizabeth, herself a part-time teacher of art at the same school. At first their parents had been entertained and delighted by the inseparability of their two middle children. Later, it had grown to irritate Mr. Musing, and he never passed up an opportunity to make what invariably proved to be a futile attempt to cast suspicion on the intimacy they shared, motivated, as his children ultimately realized him to be, not by a real feeling that what joined them was any unwholesome or ill-boding affection, but simply by jealousy of the emotional independence of his offspring and their ability to make do with each other's company rather than aspiring to his own. Mrs. Musing, as it turned out, was inclined to support them, if somewhat furtively given the facts of her husband's temperament, in their youthful and completely innocent bonding. And so, thanks to their mother, Antigone, now twenty-nine, and her older brother, thirty-one, would never feel completely alone or without friends and protection in the world, a guarantee which was the foundation and prototype of any confidence either of them could be said to have.

And so it was the arrival of her oldest friend that Antigone anticipated in her glazed alcove in her picturesque faculty home. A superficially satisfied observer might assume that it was the very closeness of the siblings that made Hiawatha's visit the calming prospect that it was, but as we have explained, Antigone was still, though by no means calm. The fact is, when we find ourselves with even the most beloved members of our families, or for that matter anyone meaningful from our distant pasts, they tend to represent to us not only themselves, purely and simply, but also whole worlds, worlds which we may happily have shared with them once upon a time, but which include other characters and events beyond our editorial control. So it was inevitable that Hiawatha would bring with him not only his lecture notes—for he, too, was a college professor, and the lecture was his ostensible reason for coming to Clare from his own campus outside Chicago—his clean shirts and his old, striped-silk bathrobe and the various medicaments to which he was so comically addicted, but also the rest of the family, invisible perhaps, but hardly possible to overlook.

While Antigone rested in her window seat, pondering and even savoring a feeling of isolation which she knew from experience would vanish when her brother arrived, she also braced herself for the memories he would unintentionally stir up in his wake. If she was outwardly relaxed, then, it was for the same reason that common knowledge tells us to make ourselves limp during a fall, that is, in order to lessen the likelihood of serious damage.

Meanwhile, serving to indicate the affinities that held them together, Hiawatha was subject to much the same thoughts as his sister. His posture at this particular moment, however, in no way resembled hers. He sat stiffly upright in the front passenger seat of the taxi on his way from the train station, a station in a neighboring town, since generations of the conservative authorities who ran Clare College and, traditionally though unofficially, the town of Westerly where it was to be found, had never allowed a train stop—that dreaded symbol of post-Enlightenment displacement and a constant reminder of alternatives to stationary scholastic pursuits—to be erected there. He, like Antigone, was only vaguely conscious of the deeper sources of his anxiety, buried as these were beneath the very genuine excitement he felt at being reunited with his favorite sibling. He ran his fingers through his glossy but thinning hair, as though resigned to, and even willing to spur on, the loss of it. He was, more obviously than Antigone, a worrier. At this moment, his need to worry focused, for lack of anything more important, on the length of the trip in the taxi and the mounting cost of the ride. He wondered to himself why he had insisted that Antigone not come to the train station to fetch him, why he had decided to start his visit with this show of self-sufficiency. He strained his eyes through that half-light that signals the approach of evening, in order to make out what he hoped would be the nearby outlines of the college buildings. He was just in the process of transferring his worries from the cost of the transportation to the more serious matter of the content of his upcoming lecture—entitled "The Ghost of the Painter, Titian, in the Cantos of Ezra Pound"— when the sound of sirens pierced the air, momentarily distracting both himself and his driver, though clearly the noise came from some distance away.

And here, prior to the actual meeting of brother and sister, was a preliminary moment of contact between them. For what Hiawatha heard, Antigone saw from her window seat: a procession, as it seemed, of three police cars and an ambulance, making its way to the northernmost corner of the campus, where the old Vanderlyn mansion stood, with all that remained of its former prestige as one of the most elegant eighteenth-century houses in the vicinity of the college. In recent years it had fallen into disrepair and seemed bound for demolition until, last February, the college had purchased it and then announced plans to renovate and transform it into a club for distinguished alumni. Perhaps one of the workmen has been injured, thought Antigone, her eyes following the flashing red lights and coming to rest with them in the general area of the house. Her speculation was suddenly brought to an end when, with a little start, she reacted to the sound of footsteps on the porch, and the doorbell rang.

II

PROFESSOR CORNELIUS VANDERLYN REACHED WITHOUT curiosity for the telephone receiver, and was mildly surprised to hear the voice of Theodore Trowbridge, president of Clare College, at the other end of the line. Very brief greetings were exchanged before Trowbridge undertook to explain the motive for his call.

"Listen, Van, the reason I had no choice but to disturb you at home was to let you know that something's happened up at your old house." There was a very pregnant pause before he added, "Something bad."

At the mention of "his old house," Cornelius, or Van, as others referred to him, felt the shell of his usual indifference to the world around him tremble slightly, though it did not actually crack. At least not immediately.

"What do you mean? Has someone been hurt? I did warn you all, before the College bought the place, that the foundations have needed work for years. What exactly has happened?" This was quickly becoming the longest extracurricular conversation that Cornelius had had in years.

"No, no. It isn't the foundations, or at least there's no problem with the work, and none of the men has been hurt. But it seems they've found something." As though impatient with his own habitual noncommittal rhetoric—that rhetoric so vital to the obtaining and maintenance of positions of power, but which also renders the speaker an ineffectual babbler when it comes to the necessity of actual communication— Trowbridge burst out, in something of his pre-presidential, human tone of voice. "They've found a body. A human body. The police want both of us to meet them there. Right now."

Cornelius reeled at the unbelievable news, and then the shell not only cracked, it disintegrated. He found himself vitally interested. "What are you saying? Whose body?!"

"Van, try to be calm. Can you meet me at the house right now? The police will be able to explain.

Look, if you need, I can pick you up on my way, but it would probably be better if you came on your own. All right? I'll see you there in fifteen minutes."

Cornelius felt disturbed, more deeply disturbed than he had been by anything in the past several years, but not so completely out of his mind with amazement as not to notice that the president hadn't given any reason for thinking it more advisable that the two men arrive at the old house separately. Cornelius was an extremely intelligent man and, given the great deal he knew of the history of human loyalties, had a tendency to be suspicious of almost everyone around him. *In a crisis, each to his own corner*—that would be the attitude of Trowbridge, who was, after all, compared to Cornelius, a parvenu to the gentlemanly world of academic power and prestige.

Despite his internal alarm, Cornelius did not jump up from his leather armchair, flinging the open *Cambridge Journal of Archeology* off his lap and tipping over the glass of bourbon on the little table at his elbow. Instead, he sat still for a moment, and tried to collect his racing thoughts. His calm exterior—comparable, if only at this particular moment, to that of the young professor of chemistry who has already been introduced but whom Professor Vanderlyn had never met— the deliberation and apparent hesitation behind his movements, expressed the habits of a lifetime, habits which had become even more marked during the last decade. When he did move, it was always meaningfully, even with grace. Now, for a period of two or three minutes, Cornelius Vanderlyn was perfectly still, his fine, fiftyish head with silver at the temples looking like a good specimen of a Roman republican bust, a senator, perhaps, but not an arrogant one, nor one whose thoughts could ever be deciphered by even the most insightful observer.

Professor Vanderlyn's surroundings spoke more eloquently of his life than he himself would ever have done aloud. These were comfortable, to say the least, a large apartment on the second floor of the prettiest of three college residential quadrangles, this one known as the Orrery, or "Ory Quad," after the old bronze model of the solar system which formed the base of the weather vane perched at its highest point. The furniture and books, the old pictures of scenes in Italy and Greece and the older rugs with their warps exposed but their beauty undiminished, the little terra-cotta vessels with traces of writing or the rubbed profiles of once-living faces, all these had been brought together from a variety of far-flung sources. Many he had moved from the old house, long before he had sold it to the college. Others he had accumulated while on digs in the Mediterranean, during his younger days, when he was still interested and active in the field. And a few were gifts from former students, several of whom, over the past twenty years, had gone on to make their own contributions to the archeological discipline. It was these gifts that Professor Vanderlyn cherished most among the ornaments and mementos that filled his collegiate abode, not so much because they had been tokens of generosity and lasting friendship as because they spoke of other people's pasts rather than his own.

Cornelius Vanderlyn's past was, superficially and with one notorious exception, a charmed one. In the first place, as a member of the Vanderlyn family, he belonged to Clare College and had been raised to believe that Clare College, to a large degree, belonged to him. For if Clare could be said to have a first family, few could have rivaled the Vanderlyn claim. A Vanderlyn had been among the four divines who had founded the college upriver of Westerly in 1676. That minister's son had been the first teacher of logic at the college and had, in fact, lost his life to a raiding party of Wampanoag Indians when he refused to cancel his classes despite confirmed rumors of their approach. And to the company of the founder and his martyr son came numerous other Vanderlyns, each playing a prominent role in the academic, as well as the economic, existence of the school. In the 1790's, for example, no fewer than three Vanderlyns served simultaneously on the faculty, at the same time that a collateral Vanderlyn, who had himself married a cousin and reassumed his wife's maiden name, was contributing the funds to raise the first of the Federal style quadrangles. Most sumptuous (and clearly labeled) of all was the legacy of Vanderlyn Brooks Vanderlyn, who, at the end of the nineteenth century—and a term as college president which certain of his contemporaries felt had seemed almost as long—commissioned and paid for the new chapel, a lofty brick structure filled with intricate wood carvings and even more stunning stained glass by both Tiffany and La Farge.

The tradition of Vanderlyns at Clare has continued well into our own day, despite occasional mumblings in the latter half of the century about nepotism. The fact remains that numerous members of the family have been excellent scholars and unquestionably deserving of their appointments at the school. Cornelius himself was the only child of famous faculty, a man-and-woman archeological team who had brought renown to Clare in the fifties. The pair had married late; Cornelius was born, after a series of miscarriages, when his determined mother was forty-two and his less determined father, fifty. Shortly after their retirement, his parents had died in quick succession, in fact, within a single year, his father of a stroke at eighty, his mother two months later of a similar attack. At the time of his parents' deaths Cornelius was completing his graduate work in the same field as theirs at the University of Chicago. When he received his doctorate in 1979, the college offered him a tenure-track position as much out of a feeling of familial obligation as due to his own scholarship, though the latter was, by any estimation, first-rate.

And now Cornelius found himself—conscientiously on foot due to the fact that he had remained in his apartment long enough after the president's call to finish his drink—making his way back to the house he had grown up in, and to which, upon his marriage, he had returned from a brief stay in Boston to live with his lovely, but altogether unfathomable, wife only two years after beginning his career at Clare. To refer to Virginia Vanderlyn, née-Scott, as an enigmatic beauty is hardly to do her justice with respect to either her looks, which were ravishing and unforgettable, or her power to mystify, which, after you had been knocked to the ground by her appearance, finished you off and dragged you away in whatever direction she happened to be going. It is possible that, prior to the advent of the English usurpers, the Indians had produced such a beauty, but one thing was certain: in the three centuries since that time, the region around Westerly had never seen such a woman as Virginia

Vanderlyn. This image, which has not been exaggerated, explained the young professor's original unquenchable attraction to her and was the image he continued to carry with him, despite the traumatic extinction of his affection, during the ten years since she had left him.

Without denying her physical appeal, many people, women especially, had naturally formed more temperate assessments of Virginia. It is inevitable that a flawless exterior gives rise to deep suspicions concerning the character of the individual thus favored. With her smooth, black, shoulder-length hair, her light blue eyes and perfect teeth, her finely turned frame, her instinct for clothes, you knew she had to be bad, and this sentiment had been expressed frequently and always *ad alta voce* by Amanda Clovis Carmichael Hughes, the most voluble faculty wife at Clare. Whether or not Virginia was as promiscuous as her husband's colleagues hoped and their wives feared, it was not so many years after the Vanderlyn marriage and the birth of their only child that Cornelius actually made an untimely and unsuspecting midday appearance at his house, to be greeted in the bathroom by his wife and an untenured English professor stepping together out of the shower. And so Virginia had been the perpetrator and subject—both the director and the star—of the one scandalous episode in Cornelius' life, that solitary lapse of the painter's attention to detail that proves the vessel a fake. But it was only solitary in the sense that she had been found out. The final disintegration of his marriage, marked by his wife's departure, took place not immediately but after several reconciliations which, to be fair, he had practically forced upon her, so in love had he been. Her faithlessness remained behind her; it was the one devastating truth he had known, far deeper than anything he had ever experienced on his digs at Paestum or Aegina. And like salt on silver, it ate into him, and could never be stopped in its course, nor ever repaired.

Now, as he passed the solemn, unspeaking faces of policemen stationed outside and mounted the stone steps toward the only house that had ever been a home to him—for his move to the college had been made only weeks after his wife had left him, and however comfortably he had arranged the apartment, he knew that it would never be, in any real sense, his home—he tried to clear his mind of all memories of his married life. But this was an almost impossible task in even the calmest of circumstances. There were many ways in which Virginia had guaranteed that her husband would continue to think of her long after she had abandoned him. The wording of her farewell note, for one, had worked upon him in the manner of a Shakespearean curse or spell, filled as it was with vague half-promises of a possible return. And the most effective and unavoidable reminder of all was, of course, their eight-year-old child, Charles, whom, without commenting upon him in her lengthy last epistle, she had left behind as well. Nevertheless, as Cornelius crossed the wide wooden veranda which had been added to the facade of the house in the late nineteenth century, he was, for the briefest moment, spared all thoughts of his adult life. Instead, from the innumerable remembered and forgotten passages over that same front porch that he had made throughout his fifty-two years, it was a very early experience that his subconscious chose to conjure up now.

He was ten years old. It was a cold February day, and the landscape of Westerly and the rooftops of Clare lay hushed under deep snow. Cornelius, swaddled in wool scarves and shiny leggings, had been playing his favorite winter game, which he called Grave Circle, the purpose of which was to find and dig up a number of small figurines that his parents had purchased for him on some distant, work-related trip. Rather transparently but effectively intended to encourage the boy in what would become his lifework, the figurines were miniature reproductions in cheap metal of the best-known masterpieces of ancient Greek sculpture. As the game required, Cornelius himself had buried the

little statuettes in the snow the day before, in a pattern
which changed each time he played the game, but
which was always highly symbolic and meaningful.
On that morning something unusual happened. He
had already excavated the site, and successfully
unearthed the tiny *Mantiklos Apollo*, and the so-called
Kritios Boy, and the *Peplos Kore*, and the *Charioteer of
Delphi*. But his favorite figure, which to his young
mind was the saddest but still the most beautiful form
the world had ever produced, was the famous *Laocoön*,
representing the last high priest of Troy being dragged
with his children into Hades by a great serpent sent by
the pro-Greek gods to prevent him from warning his
countrymen of the danger of the Trojan horse. This,
the central object in his burial site, he could not find.
What he did find, upon closer scrutiny and in the
midst of increasing alarm, were footprints in the snow
leading away from the site to the house of his neighbors, the Hugheses, one of whose children was a notorious bully who had often abused the more bookish
and considerably younger and smaller Vanderlyn boy.

But it was not the particulars of the game, nor
even the terrible feeling of despair that had overcome
him when he discovered his loss, that flashed across
the professor's mind this evening. Rather, as he tra-
versed the porch toward the outer, etched-glass door
of the hall, he remembered opening the same door on

that distant day with a furious and ill-formed plan to obtain the longest and sharpest kitchen knife he could lay hold of, a knife he would immediately use to kill Walter Hughes. Of course, no such plan was carried out; his mother had stopped him, comforted him, and been especially gracious when, later in the day, Mrs. Amanda Hughes had walked over to return the piece, the latter commenting pointedly—and as though it were the only reason she had thought to right the wrong that had been committed—that she was not in the habit of allowing her own son to play with naked idols. The incident was quickly forgotten, even by Cornelius himself, until now, forty years later, he relived again the fury and passion of his juvenile resolution to be revenged. He was startled to find that the depth of his remembered feeling actually caused him to blush, just as the chief of the Westerly Police Department opened the door and extended his hand.

"You must be Professor Vanderlyn," said the policeman, in a deep and friendly tone.

Cornelius felt odd being ushered by a policeman into his former home, but he tried to hide his discomfort, and returned the greeting succinctly but not without warmth. In the large drawing room to the left of the entrance hall, he noticed President Trowbridge, expensively sheathed in a dark suit and tie, *like an undertaker*, thought Cornelius, who also speculated that the president had probably dressed in the outfit specifically to deal with the police. It was, after all, his own uniform of sorts.

"I'm Chief Richard Staves of the Westerly Police Department. I understand this used to be your house some years ago?"

Cornelius looked without blinking into the smiling face of the other man, who was about his own age, clean-shaven, and neatly, but unofficially, attired.

"Yes, it's been in my family since it was built, around 1760."

"But you sold it to the college. When was that?"

Cornelius told Mr. Staves that he had sold the house over four years ago, but that the college had only recently purchased it from a realtor. He was still looking in the direction of President Trowbridge, who, in the middle of his own dialogue, raised both his head and a hand to Cornelius to signal hello. *How serious he looks*, thought Cornelius, before turning back to the police chief and adding, "It was much too big and dilapidated for us. After all, there's only me and my son. My son Charles. He's a student now at Clare. He lives in a dormitory. I suppose you could say that I do, too. We moved out when he was still a boy."

While Cornelius was speaking, the policeman listened thoughtfully, but said nothing. To fill the pause,

Cornelius finally added, "None of us was particularly happy here."

Still the police chief remained silent. Then rather abruptly, but still very cordially, he put his hand on the professor's arm, and said, "I suppose you know why we've had to bring you out here."

Another pause, which Cornelius again broke.

"Well, President Trowbridge told me you'd found a body. I'm hoping it wasn't some poor tramp who got buried under the house. I warned both the realtors and the college that the southeast corner of the first floor has been giving way for years."

Staves stroked his chin—a bit theatrically, thought Cornelius—and finally responded.

"Well, first of all, it wasn't technically a body that we found. It was a skeleton. A woman's skeleton. Not a great deal left to go by, but that much we know already. And secondly, it wasn't discovered in the southeast corner of the cellar, but buried in the opposite corner."

"Buried?" said Cornelius, feeling suddenly light-headed and weak on his legs.

"That's right. Buried." Then Chief Staves leaned closer to Cornelius, not at all threateningly, but quite obviously with the intention of sharing a confidence. "I'm afraid it's even worse than that," he murmured. "The visible evidence suggests that she was buried alive."

During these last pronouncements, Staves had been ushering the professor subtly but deliberately toward a window with a broad sill in the same room that the president was in. The professor and the policeman sat down, the former in something of a sick, delirious haze, before the latter continued.

"Look, I hate to make this difficult for you, but there was some jewelry among the bones. Actually, only one piece. We weren't lucky enough to find a wedding ring or anything like that—you know, the sort of thing that's usually inscribed. But I wonder, before we send the remains—the teeth and such, you understand—to be examined, I wonder if you'd have a look at this, and tell me if it rings any bell at all. Sergeant."

Staves beckoned to a uniformed policeman waiting at the entrance to the room. Cornelius looked beyond him as he approached, and saw distinctly, as though mention of them had echoed softly throughout the house, summoning them up from the subterranean cellar and into the dim light of the world, the remains of a skeleton. These were still embedded in a thick layer of earth, the entire specimen filling a long tray covered with clear plastic and perched awkwardly on a stretcher or gurney guided by two gloved officers toward the front door of the mansion. Cornelius was relieved to find that in this brief glimpse he had registered no recognition of the bones as being those of a body. They seemed very remote from anything organic, much less human.

Meanwhile, Police Chief Staves had taken from his officer a small plastic bag, which he held up for Cornelius to see. Cornelius moved his head closer to the little conglomeration of gold and colorless, faceted stone, as he habitually did with the artifacts he found on his own excavations. Then he raised his right hand to his mouth to stifle something between a gasp and a moan that nevertheless escaped him.

So she had made the promise, and kept it, too. Virginia Vanderlyn had come back.

III

S O. HAVE YOU SPOKEN TO MOM AND DAD RECENTLY?"
Antigone did her best to sound casual, even disinterested. She knew that nothing could be more natural than discussing relatives while clearing away the
dinner plates. Nevertheless, she was careful to keep
moving back and forth from the table—rearranging
the salt and pepper shakers, and symmetrizing the
candlesticks they had used to celebrate their
reunion—so that her brother should not easily be able
to catch her eye.

"Yes, very recently. I mean, last Christmas counts
as recently, doesn't it?" Hiawatha, as it turned out,
was as happy to avoid eye contact as Antigone. He

studied the little ball of beeswax he was molding between his fingers.

Antigone winced inwardly at the idea that ten months had passed since her brother had spoken to their parents. She understood his reasons, perhaps, but as all academics know, understanding something rarely makes it easier to swallow.

"I spoke to them last week. Dad sounded miserable." Antigone made one last infinitesimal adjustment to a candlestick, and then sat back down. Hiawatha's reaction was immediate. He sprang up from the table and headed through the low, cream-colored arch into the sitting room.

"How can anyone be unhappy in this day and age, when there are so many channels to choose from?"

Tig followed her brother into the other room, where he was sprawling on a chintz-covered sofa and had already used the remote control button to turn on the TV. Like most intellectuals, and everyone else in their family, Antigone had a relationship with television that was far more hate than love. Their mother never watched much, their father, though claiming to abhor it, nevertheless was capable of sitting in front of it for hours at a time, changing channels every two or three minutes and cursing in between, and their other siblings, the oldest girl, Flannery, and the youngest,

Jane, were far too preoccupied with financial concerns and social climbing, respectively, to waste much time on anything else. Hi was the exception to the rule, hedonistically and unashamedly indulging in it as an alternative to real life. He could, as Antigone was well aware, recite entire teleplays from his favorite episodes of *I Love Lucy* and *The Simpsons*.

"Yes," Antigone responded. "Just when you think you've seen every possible configuration of every plot on every program, they come along and rearrange it again. It's like the loaves and the fishes."

"Speaking of the loaves and fishes," said Hi, without looking up, "you know, that happened to me once. With shampoo. I had run out of shampoo—I mean, the bottle was empty. And I kept forgetting to buy more. But every morning in the shower . . . sure enough, there was always a little bit left. That went on for months. It was a miracle."

Before Hi could proceed to even more outlandish examples and conclusions of the parable, Tig interrupted him. "Oh, Hi, whatever would you be doing with shampoo?" She perched herself on the arm of the settee and teasingly ran her hand once over the back of her brother's thinning blond hair. With this, the first actual physical contact between them—for Musings never embraced when they met—Tig felt that it was good to see him.

Hi frowned, and his sister turned to the television screen. Her brother was about to speak, but she halted him.

"Wait a minute. Turn it up."

Hi complied, and they both stared at the image before them, of a newswoman who might actually have been nice-looking underneath and behind the jet-black polyurethane wig and teethcaps typical of the television commentator. She was standing in front of a building which Antigone instantly recognized as the Vanderlyn mansion, expounding on a terrible event in the nasal, urgent, but at the same time non-committal, tone common to all newscasters, and exaggerated in the local variety.

" . . . College officials have expressed horror and dismay at the discovery and pledged their support of a police inquiry. The remains of the body have been tentatively identified as those of Virginia Vanderlyn, former wife of well-known Clare College archeologist, Cornelius Vanderlyn. There are also rumors, as yet unconfirmed, that evidence suggests the deceased was buried alive . . . ."

"Aren't we all?" asked Hiawatha rhetorically, turning back to his sister, who seemed really shocked by the news.

"Good heavens!" exclaimed Tig, and the expression sounded terribly old-fashioned on her lips, which made Hi smile, because it had long been a shared habit of brother and sister to use, and to admire the use by others of, old-fashioned phrases.

"I can't believe it," she continued, at last slipping onto the sofa next to Hi. "I have Charlie Vanderlyn in my freshman class. He's a really strange kid. Very good-looking, but the moodiest boy I've ever seen. He always comes into class a few minutes late, sometimes whistling and clearly on a high. I don't mean on drugs, just on a lark. Other times he enters the auditorium with a scowl, kicking the furniture and slamming his books down on his desk. My God! That must be his mother!"

"Who?" asked Hi, impressed by his sister's obviously genuine interest.

"Virginia Vanderlyn. The wife of Cornelius Vanderlyn. You know, the Vanderlyns?"

"Intimately," quipped Hi. "Newport. Positano. Cap Ferrat."

Antigone paid no attention to her brother's sarcasm, but continued to fill him in on the story of one of Westerly's most famous families.

"Don't play dumb. This is THE Vanderlyn family. They practically built the college. Half the family makes the money in New York—mainly banking, I think—and the other half spends it on Clare."

"And then there's our half, the half-nots." Hi was determined to leaven the conversation.

"The half-wits, you mean. Seriously, I can't believe this. And that's the notorious Virginia Vanderlyn."

"Why notorious?" Hiawatha's interest was always aroused by that particular term.

"Well, according to everybody I've ever met, she was the most beautiful, but also the wildest, woman ever affiliated with Clare. She and her husband, that man they just mentioned, lived in his family's huge old pile of a house. They had one kid—Charlie, my student, the one with Attention Seeking Disorder— but of course that makes a lot more sense now! So anyway, she was what Mom would call "restless" and Dad would call "a goddam tramp." Maybe something in between the two. In any case, she got caught. More than once, I gather. But her husband couldn't—or wouldn't—give her up. I even heard that she once spent a weekend with an undergraduate . . . a seventeen-year-old, mind you."

" Even I draw the line at that," interjected Hi, but clearly he was enthralled by his sister's story, and wished her to go on.

"A lot of it must have been made up. You know how people, especially women, I'm afraid, can be when a beauty is dropped in their midst. Like raw flesh to the lions. Or vice versa. Like the Bacchae."

"And can you blame her, if her husband was so old and had huge piles? Isn't that what you said?"

Conversations with her big brother were always like this, Hi flinging down bizarre hurdles and Tig sailing nimbly over them. He was a satyr, she, a gazelle. There was a deep harmony between them, but neither would have fared well if left to those same maenads mentioned above.

Antigone had more to tell, and her brother was actually becoming more and more interested. He poured out the rest of the champagne he had brought—she had purchased the meal ready-made, and it had been delicious, while he had contributed a bottle of Mumm's Special with the pink foil label, because as everyone in the family had heard him declare on countless occasions, champagne was the only alcoholic drink that didn't give him a terrible stomachache afterward—and she completed her account of what she knew or had heard about the wide-ranging Vanderlyn ménage.

"Well, at last, after several years and the birth of one son, Charlie, she finally ran away. At least that's what everybody assumed. I mean, I know she left a long farewell note, not a suicide note or anything like that. And I'm sure somebody told me that she kept writing to the boy. Poor kid. Maybe I should go back and raise his quiz score. He only got a C, but I think, under the circumstances, a B- would be allowable."

It may shock the ingenuous reader, but Hiawatha, who was, after all, a young teacher like his sister, though in a very different field, only nodded his agreement when she considered aloud the change of poor young Vanderlyn's grade. For he, too, had occasionally found himself swayed in his professional assessments—and, in general and except among the most arrogant instructors of the discipline, English literature is an area of study far more open to subjective evaluation than chemistry. Consequently, each year, one or two students passed his difficult course on nineteenth-century narrative techniques based more on their ability to recount with deceptive immediacy and moving conviction a tragic incident they had never experienced than on their actual performance in written assignments. But—and this held true for both Hi and Tig—woe to those whose dishonesty was discovered. In one extreme situation, Hi had even traveled a hundred miles with a bad head cold—being sick always made him cranky, and being cranky made him suspicious—to stake out what was supposed to be the funeral service of the grandmother of a student. After some investigation, and a long talk in person with the charming old lady herself, they agreed between them that her grandson must receive a failing grade for the course immediately upon return from his six-day weekend on the eastern shore of Lake Michigan.

"Well, you must point out the place to me while I'm here. And the kid, too. Have you met the father?" Hi's natural curiosity, which was another trait common to both siblings but which, especially in Hi, could easily devolve into nosiness (though he was fond of defending himself from the accusation by reminding people that Matthew Arnold identified curiosity as the root of all culture), was becoming aroused. In the middle of his sister's negative reply to the question concerning Cornelius Vanderlyn, Hiawatha jumped up again from the couch and abruptly changed the direction of the conversation.

"Good grief! I've got to go and have a look at my lecture notes. However did I get myself into this dreadful thing?"

"What exactly is this paper you're giving?" asked Antigone, rising herself and collecting their empty glasses.

"Well, it's a conference on revivalisms in poetry. Later poets looking back and adapting forms and subjects from earlier writers. But I applied mainly so that I could come to see you." Hiawatha paused to make a sentimental cow face, then continued. "And

I've been very clever about the whole thing. I've gotten money from my department to pay for the trip. After all, my giving a lecture at Clare College is a good thing for them, too. And I'm taking off three class days, so I can stay with you right through Thanksgiving. That's correct, almost two weeks together. You lucky you, you."

Antigone listened to her brother as he relived once again the original thrill of his coup, culling professional development funds to pay for his extended vacation. She was already aware, of course, of the intended length of his visit, and was herself glad for it, because this would give her an opportunity to convince her brother to come home with her for Thanksgiving, something he would assuredly not be doing without her sisterly pressure and possibly still not doing with it.

Conducting her brother to the guest bedroom, and watching him unpack his battered leather suitcase, which had been their grandfather's, she questioned him once again.

"But what are *you* talking about?"

"Ghosts. Not the Ibsen play, but the ghosts of Renaissance painters in the poetry of Ezra Pound."

Antigone leaned against the doorjamb, recognizing the bathrobe that her brother removed from among his things. And underneath it were the little plastic bottles of pills. She was tired suddenly, and a bit distracted.

Hi turned to look at her.

"You are coming, aren't you? I told someone named Randall Ross, who's the organizer of the conference, that I would bring a guest to the dinner afterward. Didn't you say you knew him?"

Tig's mind was elsewhere; nevertheless, she responded with warmth. "Oh yes, I'll be there."

Then the brother and sister said good-night, and Tig made her way down the hall to her own room, thinking aloud but in a whisper, "Speaking of ghosts. Poor Charlie Vanderlyn!"

IV

October 11, 1989

D EAR VAN,
   *I know that you already know what I am going to
say. But still I'm afraid of repeating a lot of old clichés.
You're worth so much more than that, and, you've helped
me to see, so am I. But despite all your efforts, I'm still no
smarter in your way than I was when you met me. I am
a failed experiment. It isn't all my fault, as you know. I
used to think it wasn't your fault at all, but now I think
differently. Your persistence with me, and your absolute
refusal to let me go—however pitiful that may be—is a
force that you use against me. I suppose it was flattering*

at first, but now it disgusts me. Maybe I shouldn't even be writing this down.

So I'm leaving you. And I'm leaving you in the only way I can trust myself to do it, like a coward, behind your back, by letter rather than face to face, because I know now that I will always be too weak to walk away from you in person. Probably this means I still love you. If I do, it is a rare quality in me. But our marriage is over. I'm sure we should never have been married in the first place, and one of the things I regret most is that I didn't hold out longer, or refuse you altogether. You will never deny that I did try to avoid the whole thing. I'm not the kind of woman who should be married, because if I weren't, I'm sure I wouldn't seem so bad. To myself, I mean, because as you know, I don't give a damn about your colleagues and so-called friends. They were never colleagues or friends to me. Their cruelty, or the occasional kindness I found among the small minority, meant nothing to me after my first few weeks at Clare.

Do you remember in Rome, once, shortly after we were married, you took me to some museum or other where there was a famous picture by Caravaggio? I think it was Judith Beheading Holofernes—you'll correct me if I'm wrong—but right this minute that picture comes into my mind. Judith—if she is Judith—is sawing that man's head off, but it's pretty obvious she doesn't want to. Or at least, it makes her sick. You're no enemy as Holofernes was to Judith, but I do feel that's what I've been doing to you for years, breaking off pieces of you, and you won't even help me to stop. You just lie there, in love, and bleed.

There's only one way to make it stop, and that's by going away. I don't know for how long. Probably forever. But I do know that it's got to be far away from here, and I don't want you to try and get in touch with us, at least for awhile. I'll get in touch with you, when I'm ready. In the meantime, don't believe everything that you hear about me, or should I say "fear" about me? One day you'll look back on this and thank me. Maybe then you'll see it was the only time I showed any self-control.

Yours, as they say,

Virginia

P.S. Chuck is coming tomorrow to put in the new boiler, and there are frozen steaks and shrimp in the fridge. Eat and don't worry; it may take a long time, but we'll definitely end up all right.

Virginia Vanderlyn drummed her crimson finger-nails against the vanity, letting the ink dry before folding up the letter. Automatically studying herself in the mirror, she looked now for some slight change, a sign in her own features to confirm that she was finally doing the right thing. For everyone concerned. But there was only the same look of aloofness, that well-chiseled and attractive expression that expressed nothing. Her husband was not the first or the last man who had fallen in love with that look, mistaking the mask for the wearer. And even when, finally, he came to see that it was a mask, he seemed unable to grasp that it was not the product of her art, concealing depths of character and intention that were consistent with the level established by her outer beauty.

Cornelius thought he could mine her, but what he brought up was fool's gold. Then he thought he could teach her, but she proved the one student beyond his power to enlighten and guide. Finally he tried, out of desperation—after even *he* must have known it was too late—to remake her. And everything went smash.

This letter, which she now folded in two and placed upright, like the dessert menu in a diner, against the mirror in what, until this moment, had been *their* bedroom, was the most difficult thing she had ever had to write. Her many detractors would have added that it was probably the longest as well. She had pondered it, literally, for years. Now she had serious doubts as to its adequacy. It was not as apologetic as she intended it to be. But then, neither was it as angry as it ought honestly to have been. Ultimately, many of the emotions she meant to put in it had cancelled each other out. She might not be an academic, but she had a good brain. And she recognized that this letter fell far short of being even the tip of an iceberg of an explanation.

Still, there wasn't time for revision, much less reconsideration. She glanced at the clock on the table at her side of the bed, a face which had become as familiar to her as her own during long nights of quiet wakefulness, with her husband sleeping innocently beside her. One thing she could never escape was the feeling that she did not belong here. Cornelius fit the place—the house, the college—like a piece of custom-built furniture. But she was a jarring lapse of venerable taste. It had taken her two years to unpack her limited number of pre-marital possessions, and long after the birth of Charlie she continued to expect the arrival at her bedroom door of a concierge inquiring as to the length of her stay.

Virginia was wracked by a momentary shiver, one of those involuntary bodily movements that indicate aversion to a particular train of thought. Never one to dwell on even the most recent events of her past, she quickly transferred her attention to the practical aspects of her departure. Opening the drawers of the vanity, she hastily gathered up all the personal items necessary to the perpetuation of her infamous natural beauty. She herself smiled at the irony of this, but didn't waste valuable packing time developing the paradox, the way Cornelius's colleagues might have done. If, as we have seen, Virginia was no scholar, if, in fact, she was the antithesis of her husband in this, it was because, above all, she knew the proper value of a surface, but never mistook it for the substance. In other words, Virginia understood both the work that went into creating someone like herself, and also how little such effort actually—on the most important level—mattered. She neither underrated nor overrated herself or others, and so she was a threat to, if not positively murder on, her college acquaintances. It could have been worse, she knew; she might have married a diplomat, and that would probably have resulted in political assassinations, if not outright war.

Virginia brightened at the passing notion of problems bigger than her own. Then, laying both hands flat against the dressing table as an outward manifestation of recharged resolve, she launched herself upward to a standing position, and swiftly scanned the room. In a moment she was rifling the closet, weeding out every third or fourth blouse or skirt, things she hadn't worn in years, leaving them in a rising heap of colored fabric under her left arm. These she would drop off at the Catholic church. She chose that particular denomination not only because the Vanderlyn family were notorious Episcopalians, but also because St. Mary's was just down the road from Charlie's school. Next, in what may have seemed the reverse of the natural order, she used both arms to scoop together all of the far greater number of remaining garments—clothes were, after all, one, if not the only, key to both her confidence and her survival—and with striking agility (when had she done this before?) unhooked their hangers and deposited them *en masse* on the bed beside two large, gaping suitcases.

Fortunately for Virginia, she had already foreseen and braced herself for this, the moment she dreaded most, when, as had happened more than once in her late teens and early twenties, she was forced to stand over and contemplate the small pile of things that were the sum total of her physical existence. She had no black leather cases bulging with pearls, no heirlooms that had never left her in her wanderings. We have already seen that the furniture, to a portion of which she had at least some legal claim, had no connection to her whatever, and at any rate she would never have tried to take it with her. In fact, she wanted nothing from Cornelius beyond the small sum of money she had already withdrawn from their joint account. Even her wedding ring she had removed, quickly and automatically and as though tearing off a bandage, leaving it on the vanity next to her note. No, with respect to baggage—sentimental or resellable— she had long ago learned that the lighter you traveled, the faster and farther you were sure to go.

Virginia reflected, a little bitterly, on this fact. It was the greatest and least forgivable disservice the women at Clare had done her, the suggestion that she had ever been motivated by the desire for material gain. True, she had enjoyed the comfort—the ostensible and extremely superficial comfort—that life with Cornelius had provided her. She had eaten the expensive meals and found them pleasing, and the wines even more so, for the richness of its cellars remains one of the most private, but also one of the least controvertible, proofs of the quality of an east-coast educational institution. She had even enjoyed the trips she had taken with her husband. But he had never been for her the sort of investment that even nowadays so many women, with far better reputations than Virginia's, equated with a spouse. To begin with, Cornelius wasn't as wealthy as people tended to assume; except for the house and a relatively limited trust, his was an average middle-class estate. His own cousin, who had once offered himself to Cornelius's wife with an audacity that shocked even her, was far wealthier than Cornelius, and the cousin was by no means the richest of Virginia's pre- and post-marital suitors.

If Virginia, contemplating her limited number of worldly belongings as she thrust them, hangers and all, into her suitcases, seemed to dwell on the financial uncertainty of her future, to which these possessions to some extent necessarily alluded, it was not, then, because of personal avidity or avarice. But she could not escape the most delicate of all factors in this critical moment of decision, the person who would be most affected by her move, and that was her son, Charlie. If she was, momentarily and uncharacteristically, disturbed by her financial outlook, it was only because she wanted desperately to take good care of him. He was, after all, to use the terminology of the television courtroom, the only innocent in the whole affair. Virginia was always uncharacteristic when it involved her child; she loved him completely, even enough to be other than at heart she was. Or perhaps it was only with Charlie that she was herself, and that was why, together and without anything else, they would begin a new life.

She knew that taking Charlie away with her would be devastating for her husband. But, she reasoned, no doubt self-servingly, it would be better to leave with him now than later. If this was no life for Virginia, it was even less acceptable for her son. He represented the one good thing in her life, the only pure relationship, one which even her most imaginative critics had never dared to impugn. When in the past, and not only prior to her marriage, she had found herself in the position of uprooting, of leaving someone behind, her departure had never been impeded by the existence of a child. But during the eight years since Charlie's birth, everything had been different. At first, he was the reason she had stayed with Cornelius; now, although neither he nor his father could be expected to understand this, he was at least part of the reason she was going away. She loved him, and he was her only trustworthy motive for action.

Of course, one might have been justified in asking Virginia how, if she cared for her child so much, she had been able to continue to have affairs after his birth. Her best, if not only, friend at Clare, Hermione Pole, had even come close to pointing out this apparent contradiction during a very recent confidential discussion in the courtyard of the library. Well, Virginia didn't know how it was possible. And so she took comfort, then as now, in the dim certainty that the affairs had decreased, both in number and seriousness, since Charlie was born. Now he was her goal. She had not yet attained him, was not yet worthy of him, but working for him, toward him, would be a good reason for living, as it was for leaving.

She stood up at the end of the bed and looked back at the note. The wedding ring flashed in the sunlight and seemed to disappear. She considered snatching it up again before it was too late; after all, it might pay the rent for a month or two, allowing her to put off what she knew would be the inevitable need to write to Cornelius for help. But she decided against taking the ring, fingering instead the little diamond brooch at her throat. That was enough. With a last burst of momentum, she locked her suitcases and her heart and made her way with them and the rest of her things across the hall to the stairs.

On the landing, in front of the Serlian window, she put the suitcases down. They were heavier than she had anticipated. When she stopped, she heard a noise, as of something being broken, something wooden, in the lower regions of the house.

Was it her conscience rattling?

She was both miserable and elated, for she realized that, after all, she did have one.

V

TO AN OBSERVER WHO HAD NO FAMILIARITY WITH him, Hi might have seemed to be in some sort of physiological distress. He was practically hyperventilating, and he himself could see his heart pounding through the three layers of his undershirt, shirt, and jacket. To his own eye, the red silk tie he was wearing bobbed up and down. He would have liked something to drink, even a sponge dipped in vinegar. If he had dared to swallow a pill now, it would have rebounded out of his mouth to the furthest corner of the room. It was, in any case, too late to think of tonics. His introduction was almost over.

"And we are very proud to have lured so promising a young scholar to Clare to speak to us today on 'The Ghost of the Painter, Titian, in the Cantos of Ezra Pound.'"

An elegant man, with jet-black hair and a figure that seemed to belie his forty-eight years, turned with a welcoming gesture from the podium to where Hiawatha slouched uncomfortably in his corner chair. The elegant man was Randall Ross, a well-known and very active member of the English Department at Clare and of the larger academic community as well. Professor Ross had organized this conference and had been pleased to include a number of younger speakers on a wide range of topics. His own area of scholastic research was the Augustan poets, and he had already delivered the opening paper on "Ancient Patterns in the Works of Pope."

Hiawatha, who, after a little pause, stood up and approached the makeshift dais, was the second from last speaker of the day. Only he knew that if he had been earlier in the program, as originally planned, he would surely have been gone by now.

Antigone, of course, might also have known. She sat toward the back of the room, which was one of the most beautiful on the Clare campus, though it was also, without doubt, the worst suited to academic presentations. Known as the Dutch Salon, it had been removed in its entirety from a seventeenth-century manor house outside of Amsterdam. Purchased and presented to the college by some benefactor or other in the last century—a Vanderlyn or a Brooksfield or a Hughes—it had been reassembled on the top floor of Hever Hall, where the English Department had its offices. Small and almost completely windowless, its dark walls were covered in linen-fold paneling, with masterful carvings of real and fantastic animals at various intervals in the woodwork. Today, as often in the past, it was arranged like a formal classroom, with a small platform at one end, and six rows of armless oak chairs crowded into the remaining area.

Antigone was familiar with the room, as she was with Randall Ross. In fact, she had come to know both of them at the same time, when the two colleagues had served on a committee which met regularly here during the previous year. Though she did not know Ross well enough to consider him a friend, exactly, she did respect his energy and integrity and was very pleased when Hiawatha had told her that he had applied to give a talk at a conference instigated by the English professor.

The conference itself, however, was hardly pleasant for Antigone. She looked down again at the program, which had made both her and Hiawatha laugh over the breakfast table that morning. The cover was emblazoned with the title of the proceedings: Conference on Revivalism and Poetics. "Crap," as Hiawatha had gleefully noted, explaining further that Ross himself had written a letter apologizing for the implied acronym, an oversight of the college printer who had jumped the gun and titled the conference himself. While the witlessness of the printer was beyond suspicion, the participants in the conference were prodigiously amused, each speaker feeling it incumbent upon him or herself to make some reference to it in their respective preliminary remarks. Antigone was confident—and subsequently relieved—that Hiawatha would make no such reference, though as of this moment, he had done nothing but say thank you and swallow the entire glass of water on the podium.

Antigone had come to hear Hiawatha, who had originally been scheduled as the third speaker of the day. For that reason, she had shown up for part of the morning session as well. And she had tried to appear interested in the papers. But she was disappointed from the very start. She had, for example, assumed that her colleague Professor Ross's paper on "Ancient Patterns" would involve a slide show on eighteenth-century wallpapers. But no such diversion was provided. After the third paper, and after being assured by her brother that his own talk had been moved to the late afternoon, she had been happy to leave the

Dutch room for her own more modern classroom in the science building. It was not at all that she wasn't literary, but fiction was her true love. Poetry left her either unmoved or angry. On the other hand, she and her siblings, guided by their parents, had read most of the classics of English fiction before leaving high school. She had often reflected that novels, more than anything else, were the bond that held her family together, to the extent that it was so.

Antigone, too, felt a generous, empathetic suspense as her brother began his presentation.

"Well, first of all, I'd just like to say that everyone here has left the lights on in their cars, so would you all please leave right now to remedy the situation."

Thus Hiawatha chose to begin his talk with what he privately referred to as the "Greta Garbo move," that is, the pretense of an inclination to be alone. Only Antigone knew that he wasn't pretending at all, just as she alone realized that the little icebreaker was intended to relax the speaker more than to amuse his audience. In any case, it proved effective. The room tittered with an appreciative, though for some an uncertain, chuckle, and under cover of the subsequent pause, Hiawatha was able to take a gulp of air, and launch into his presentation. What followed a rather formal preface was a series of conjectures on Hiawatha's part, paving the way to no conclusions.

Whereas all of the other speakers had read their papers,
Hi abandoned his very early on. Instead of reciting, he
meandered his way through the mind of the poet who
was his primary subject, providing by his manner a
metaphor for the way Pound himself had wandered
through the great Byzantine city of Venice, the most
illusory city in the world, which, in Hiawatha's own
words, "floats forever on the slime-darkened water-
ways, its tremulous, clanging towers and its gilded,
Oriental domes merely the mask of a living entity
obsessed, like Narcissus, with its own infinitely-
repeated reflections in the Adriatic sea and sky."

Antigone was herself nearly seduced by such passages, in which her brother dissected Canto XXV. At
the same time she could not help but notice that his
presentation differed from those of his colleagues in
more ways than one. For instance, he seemed not to
embrace his topic as wholeheartedly as the others
had theirs. Antigone knew that Hi was better when
he worked with subjects which aroused mixed emotions in him. In this sense, Pound was ideal, because
Hiawatha naturally found various aspects of the
poet's life and character repulsive, at the same time
considering that much of the poetry he had produced
was among the most beautiful in the language.
Finally, a major difference between Hiawatha's presentation and the others was that his was entirely

lacking in polish. Where his colleagues had spoken with great precision and unquestioning confidence, Hi seemed repeatedly to be groping for the right words. This reminded Tig of one or two of the best teachers they had had in college. She could not gauge the effect this would have on her fellow listeners, but she found it very moving. When he did come upon the right word, it was as though you had discovered it with him. By the end of his talk, Antigone was beaming with pride.

But just as Hiawatha was concluding his presentation, exactly thirty minutes after he had begun, he was interrupted by the sound of a door loudly banging shut, followed by an even louder shout.

"Professor Musing?!"

Both Antigone and Hiawatha instinctively froze. The audience turned with perfect synchrony toward the only entrance to the room, which was at the rear. There stood a young man, his wavy blond hair dripping with sweat, his eyes glassy and wide, his cheeks enflamed and his lips trembling.

"Professor Musing?!"

He called again, and this time his tone was at once more plaintive and more urgent, the words elongated slightly by an unmistakable drunken drawl.

After a brief quizzical glance at her brother, who seemed truly in a haze at the podium, Antigone turned around and confronted the young man. It was Charlie Vanderlyn. He had not attended her class that morning, which was hardly surprising, given the recent developments in his family, now known to all at the college and beyond. Startled by the sight of him there, Antigone felt a wrenching pity for him. With no clear plan of action, but with a hasty look of affectionate apology to her brother, she hurried from her seat and led the boy out of the room.

Once in the hallway, Charlie turned to his teacher and tried to explain his reasons for tracking her down.

"I wanted to tell you I wouldn't be in class today," he began. As class had ended three hours ago, it was a rather belated message. Suddenly Charlie looked terribly sad, and in fact, his next words were filled with remorse, as though it was only now that he realized he had just interrupted something, made a fool of himself, and embarrassed his professor.

"I'm so sorry," he said, looking toward Tig, with a face that suddenly blurred over with tears. Though it was forbidden in all of the latest handbooks on teacher-student relations, Tig put an arm around Charlie, then led him slowly toward the elevator.

"It's all right, Charlie. I really do think I understand." Antigone was moved and even a bit frightened by this strange summons, but such emotions did not show in her own features or movements. She gently guided the young man out of the building, as he sobbed, stopping occasionally to wipe his eyes and sniff.

When they reached the first arch outside the nearest quadrangle, which happened to be Ory Quad, where Charlie's father lived, she sat down on one of the two little stone benches built into the supporting walls. This was as much to collect herself as him. Charlie stood next to her, head down, in an emblematic posture of misery and defeat, though he had stopped crying and was now only irregularly shaking from the dregs of his outburst. Antigone thought she smelled alcohol, but wasn't positive. The silence spread and rose until it was finally broken, again abruptly, by the boy.

"I'm so sorry, Professor Musing. I didn't mean to embarrass you. I just wanted to explain why I couldn't come to class. I was sick. I was really sick. I didn't know what to do."

These words, and the way they were delivered between deep breaths that revealed the likelihood of more tears, also indicated that Charlie was probably still quite drunk. Antigone said nothing, but pondered a moment. She wanted very much to help the young man, who was clearly living a nightmare. Yet at the same time, she felt that it would be rude, perhaps even outrageous, to say anything to him that might seem to warrant a response. At last she decided she could at least indicate her willingness to help. She was about to make this offer when suddenly they found themselves the object of a swiftly approaching figure. It turned out to be another young man, not a student of Antigone's, but some other student whom she recognized as a frequent companion of Charles's. He came up to them and, almost without seeming to notice Antigone, wrapped both of his arms around Charlie's left arm and shoulder. The gesture was warm, but it reminded Antigone of the way Hi had been supported by orderlies after an operation he had undergone at the age of sixteen.

"Charlie, Charlie, Charlie. I've been looking for you everywhere." The other student shook his friend affectionately. "And I'm not the only one. Come on. We've got to go. It'll be all right now."

The two young men walked slowly away from Tig, who was puzzled but also a little relieved that her ability to handle situations like this had not been tested further. When necessary, in her own family, she had often risen to the level of such traumas—for there had been more than a few—and beaten them down with her reason and her great understanding. But this had taken her completely by surprise. She was just about to get up and head back to the conference, which had probably already ended, when, in the middle ground of the quadrangle, Charlie stopped and turned to her. He was unashamedly rubbing his eyes, like a child.

"So, do you think he did it?" Charlie called out. He was crying again. "Do you think my father killed my mother?"

The hour, which for the Musings had begun with Hiawatha's heart pounding as though to escape from his body, ended now with Antigone's, composed as it was of the same genetic matter, beating as furiously an inch or two above her breast.

VI

CORNELIUS PUT HIS BOOKS DOWN IN THE ENTRYWAY of his apartment and picked up the letters and messages which his cleaning lady had left on the hall table. It struck him as indescribably strange, this re-enactment of all the daily rituals of his life, many as small as, or smaller than, dropping his books and retrieving his mail, after the events of the previous day. For Cornelius, everything had changed, and not in the ways that he or anybody else might have expected.

To begin with, he experienced an eerie and illogical relief. As yet utterly unable to face the horror surrounding the manner of Virginia's death, Cornelius

focused instead on where she had been found. It was
highly ironic, under the circumstances, that the discovery of his wife's body beneath their former house
had left him feeling exonerated, like a man whose
neighbors have long regarded him as the perpetrator
of a legendary crime, who wakes up one morning to
learn that the real culprit has been in prison for years.
The inescapable fact for Cornelius was that Virginia
had never actually left him, and he could hardly bring
himself to see beyond this revelation. He had not yet
taken the time to reconsider her last letter, which,
after all, he knew by heart, in the light of the recent
discovery. When he did, it would present numerous
inconsistencies, inconsistencies which he alone
would be expected to address. At the same time, it left
no doubt that she had, in any case, *intended* to leave.
Nor had it yet dawned upon Cornelius, stunned as he
still was and living in a kind of dream, that he would
be looked upon with suspicion by even those closest to
him, including his own son.

Of course, Cornelius did think a great deal about
Charlie, whom he, very differently from Virginia but
every bit as deeply, loved and wanted to protect.
Detective Staves had taken Cornelius, at the latter's
request, directly to Charlie's dormitory after the incident the previous evening. There, the father had tried
to explain, throughout the necessary and only slightly

tempered description of the preliminary findings, that the most important thing of all, which was now suddenly plausible, was that Virginia had never left her son behind. As his father was speaking, Charlie listened, dumbfounded and stricken with a horrible feeling of nausea, a confused mixture of physical paralysis, renewed loneliness, grief, and guilt.

For Charlie's life, just like his father's, had been completely colored by the fact of his apparent abandonment by Virginia. Family, friends, and neighbors had all noticed the devastation the eight-year-old had suffered when she went away. He had, after all, been almost inseparable from her, to such a degree that the question about her which most maddened and intrigued her fellow faculty wives was how she found the time to carry on so outside of her home. "Where there's a will, there's a way," Amanda Hughes had reminded, in her owl-like manner, though that was as close as the woman would go toward treading upon the relationship of mother and son. And even Mrs. Hughes had felt a frequent tug of pity for the boy after his mother had gone.

Now eighteen, Charles Vanderlyn had the appearance of a man. But, unlike Cornelius, Charlie was still young enough, still soft enough, to remain in many ways the same creature he had been before Virginia's departure, which must hereafter be recognized as her demise. Outwardly, he had grown more and more resentful of the world around him, and gained a reputation for being hotheaded and sullen by turns—in a word, farouche. But inside, too, he had grown, and there he had never relinquished the mother he frequently claimed to despise. Only Cornelius suspected the contradiction, and the truth of the matter, that, with his wavy, dark blond hair and blue eyes and his deep interior fear of the human world, Charlie was still an innocent. An angel, but not the one by Leonardo, the one by Verrocchio, trapped between two larger beings, both of whom he would always adore.

This is by no means to suggest that Charlie was easy to get along with, even at home. He was capable of being obstinate to the point of violence, and for the reasons already made known, he was used to being indulged in this. He was, after all, a Vanderlyn. No one understood better than Cornelius that bearing a well-known and respected name may be more a burden than a blessing. It is like carrying, from birth, all the food you will ever need in life on your shoulders. One thing seems certain: you will never go hungry. But another thing is possible: you may be crushed beneath the very provisions which provoke interest and envy among those around you. Charlie was conscious of his physical security, but he also felt the emotional insecurity that is not precluded—that is, on the contrary, sometimes guaranteed—by the former.

In the daily routine of their lives since Virginia's disappearance, the relationship between Cornelius and his son might best be described as one of mutual mystification. This is, of course, often the case between parents and their children, at least when viewed by an outsider to the family, though the lack of understanding is just as frequently skin deep or at any rate relatively superficial. But the reciprocal indecipherability of the Vanderlyn males was especially profound, deepened as it had been by the departure of the wife and mother.

Only weeks after that event, Cornelius had moved with his son into the apartment he now occupied alone. He had spent a large part of the next ten years trying to free Charlie from the nightmare into which the apparent abandonment by Virginia had hurled him. He had considered leaving Westerly, of taking the boy to Chicago, where Cornelius had a standing offer of employment. Finally, he had been both saddened but optimistic when Charlie himself requested, as an alternative to such a move, to be allowed to attend, as a boarding student, St. Mark's School, two hours away in Southborough. This had led Cornelius to hope that his son would not return to Westerly for college, a hope that proved unfounded when Charlie told his father, on the very day of his graduation from high school and with the most curious blank expression on his face, that he had already been accepted by, and had every intention of enrolling at, Clare.

So now father and son were both living in Westerly again, together but not together, apart but not apart. Charlie had naturally chosen to live in a dormitory; his father accepted this as the most natural thing. But he would have liked to see more of his son. There was no pattern to their meetings or communications. It was as though their renewed geographical proximity only underlined a distance that had long separated them, even when they had shared the same roof. Cornelius had to restrain himself from exerting any pressure upon the boy, forcing himself to be content with the occasional unplanned visit or the only slightly more frequent return of a telephone call. And so, Charlie disappeared into his student life, but still hovered about his father, like someone with something to say who has no words to say it. In fact, this was the way they had been for years.

A single incident will suffice to summarize the strange quietude which marked the relationship between the father and son. When he was ten years old, Charlie had accompanied Cornelius on a brief trip to an ongoing dig at Cumae, a Greek site in southern Italy. They were staying at Naples, and one evening before sunset, while they were out walking on the busy via Toledo, which is one of the most fascinating but also most frightening streets in Europe, the excited and, by all appearances, happy, boy wandered away from his father. Frantic with the incommunicable worry that only a missing child can evoke, Cornelius raced up and down the thoroughfare, enlisting, as best he was able, the aid of six or seven policemen and scouring alone the side streets into the dangerous Quartiere Spagnuolo and the Galleria Umberto I. After nearly an hour, the worst of his life, he spotted his son at the corner of the via Trinità degli Spagnuoli. He was tightly clutching the hand of a crippled teenager, one of many young people in the city whose occupation it was to sell pirated garments from an outdoor, and easily transported, clothes rack.

Now this teenager had often been noticed by the American pair, and had been the subject of remarks made by both of them during their regular walks, stationed as he always was at the same corner, with his unusual appearance and gait. He was a striking individual, one of the strangest specimens Cornelius had come upon anywhere. About eighteen or nineteen years old, he had black hair and blacker eyes, and his face was irresistibly beautiful, but molded in such a way and covered with so perfect and translucent a skin, that he seemed almost inhuman, like a statue in

a church. In fact, what his head most resembled was
what, underneath, it was: a skull. Cornelius had once
commented, a bit absent-mindedly, that the young
man was the luckiest person alive, for he was his own
memento mori, and a hundred years after he died, he
would still look exactly the same. The antithesis of his
face, his body was a paradigm of physical imperfec-
tion. His entire left side seemed already to have died,
and he dragged it slowly about with his hardly less-
impaired right. It was in such company that Cornelius
found his son, tightly squeezing the hand of this
strange apparition; he had sought out and was now
literally clinging for life to an image of suffering and
death. And when father and son were reunited—
when they had both collected themselves (for both
were crying) and thanked the young man with a mon-
etary gift and were themselves walking back to their
hotel hand in hand—neither of them said a word. Nor
was the incident ever mentioned or alluded to at any
subsequent time.

But thoughts of his son inevitably brought him
back to his wife. Now, setting down the unscanned
letters and bills, Cornelius walked to the window of
his sitting room overlooking the quadrangle. He stared
for some time, and not without remorse for his self-
ishness, through the arch of glass, thinking to himself,
She might never have gone. His reverie was finally

interrupted when he recognized, moving slowly across the college lawn, the light blue of his son's windbreaker. The boy was apparently being supported by a friend of his, a fellow student whom Cornelius also recognized but whose name he could not, at the moment, recall. The two were making their way toward the ground floor entrance of the building where Cornelius lived.

"Poor child," the archaeologist said aloud. But then again the thought returned, *She might never have gone.*

VII

I T WAS JUST AFTER SIX P.M. WHEN A SMALL PROCESSION
of upright figures issued from the main entrance of
Hever Hall and made its way unhurriedly across the
adjoining lawn, the predominantly tweed-covered line
broken occasionally by the softer surfaces of a cotton
shirt or a silk blouse or tie. The evening was just coming on, and it promised to be a warm and lovely one.
Hiawatha, especially after the turbulence that coin-
cided with the end of his presentation, was happy
not to be engaged in any academic conversations,
though several of his fellow travelers, all of whom
were strangers to him, did stop to congratulate him on
his contribution, and at least two made sympathetic

reference to the disruption by the unruly young man, whose identity was only now being circulated among them.

They were all on their way to have drinks and dinner at the home of the organizer of the conference, Professor Ross. As he depended on staying with the group in order to find his way there, Hi's uppermost concern was with his sister and her present whereabouts. Would she have taken care of that strange situation by now, and would she be able to come to the dinner and explain everything to him when she arrived?

These questions were answered when Professor Ross himself caught up with Hiawatha and put a friendly arm on his shoulder.

"Well, Professor Musing, I thought your talk was splendid, and I'm very proud to have discovered you."

With a slight increase in the pressure on Hiawatha's arm, Randall Ross brought them both to a stop, allowing other members of the group to walk around and ahead of them. The two men looked at each other. Hiawatha always felt it difficult to accept compliments, but he did manage, in the same somewhat groping manner that had characterized his delivery from the podium, to indicate his thanks. This was, in truth, the only public manner of speaking Hiawatha had, since he was genuinely shy, even for an academic, and it was mainly for his family, and Antigone above all, that he reserved his more relaxed and facetious discourse. The older man, whose open looks and kind voice seemed in contrast made for public appreciation, continued.

"Listen, Hiawatha. What a name! I wish I had such a name, though I suppose you suffered for it as a child, eh? Your sister telephoned the department secretary and left a message that she would meet you at my house before dinner. There, she says, all will be made clear. You know, I hadn't the slightest idea that you were Antigone Musing's brother! I wish I had her name, too!"

The two men laughed, and Hiawatha was doubly gratified, because this information from his new acquaintance also cleared away the tiny worry in Hiawatha's mind that his sister had somehow been the reason his proposal had been accepted for the conference. They walked on together toward the house, Ross singing out now and then, rather inconsequentially given that the topic they were discussing was Italy, but also without seeming in the least impolite, lines which he was apparently remembering piecemeal from the famous Longfellow poem.

The house occupied by Randall Ross and his equally attractive, if less scrutable, wife Laura, was by no means among the largest in Westerly. The general appearance of the property from the front, where a low stone wall encircled a small rectangle of late-blooming flowers and lawn, was what any realtor would be justified in calling "charming," the lines of the house itself, "tidy." It was a two-story brick bungalow in the much-diluted Cotswold style, probably built, like the other houses on the same residential street, during the 1920s. When the group from the college arrived—the walk took less than fifteen minutes—they found the door wide open.

Hi experienced a familiar, and highly pleasurable, suspense upon entering the Rosses' front hall, where Professor Ross left him to look for his wife. This sense of anticipation was a legacy of Hi's early childhood, a period when his parents had often taken him and his siblings to visit their colleagues *en famille*. Even later in life, Hiawatha had once annoyed his father, who was trying to help him write his application essays for graduate school, by claiming that the only reason he wanted to go was to see the insides of faculty homes. What was merely an instance of Hiawatha's surliness nevertheless contained a modicum of truth.

He was not to be disappointed here. The Ross home was small, but beautifully decorated. There was a great deal of expensive, cream-colored paneling to be admired on the ground storey, and the furniture was all very pretty, the antiques well spaced like rare perennials in a rich man's garden. The predominant woods were walnut and mahogany, but there were also pieces overlaid with rose- and fruitwood marquetries, the fittings in gilt bronze, ivory, and bone. Most of the visible space had been arranged for the coming meal, three round tables having been set, one in the sizable drawing room, one in the dining room, and one placed directly under the low arch which marked the boundary between the two. A dignified eighteenth-century English mahogany sideboard presided over one end of the dining room, nearer the kitchen, and on it was a seductive array of hors d'oeuvres, radiating from the center, which was occupied by an oversized, export China bowl, containing punch.

When Hi entered the dining room, he saw Antigone had already arrived and was engaged in conversation with Randall Ross. She waved to Hiawatha and broke off her conversation. Moving from opposite corners of the increasingly crowded room, the brother and sister met at the punch bowl. There, they soon learned, the topic under discussion was Denton Smackey's latest book, *How to Con the People Who Love You*. Some were saying that it was the funniest satire they had read in years. Others laughingly agreed, afraid to acknowledge they had taken notes.

"Well, I'm so glad you could make it, Professor Musing," said Hi, who was immediately put at ease by his sister's presence.

"Same to you, Sunshine," was Antigone's reply.

"So tell me, dear sister of the blood, who are all these people, and what do they want from us?"

"You should know better than I. I've never seen most of them before in my life. My advice is, hold onto your purse." With this, Antigone handed Hiawatha a glass of the rum-laden punch.

"Already gone," sighed Hi, pausing briefly before launching into a barrage of questions.

"Where did you disappear to? I've been told by three different people that the student who was screaming for you at the door was the famous Vanderwho boy, son of the even more infamous Vanderwhat man. Is he your student? I think you told me he was. Do all your students cry when they see you? Is that always a good thing?"

Antigone held a glass to her lips, scanned the room with her eyes, and began her reply.

"Yes, yes, and yes."

Hiawatha waited a moment, till he was sure his sister felt him sufficiently teased, and then intoned, a bit loudly, "And?"

"First of all, I have to tell you how proud I was when you spoke. I don't know much about the topic, but I know you were wonderful." Antigone paused to let the compliment sink in, before going on. Hi only rolled his eyes, impatiently. "And yes, it was the Vanderlyn kid. Quite drunk. I changed my clothes before coming back because I think he may have doused them with his seventy-eight-proof tears. As they're bound to have candles this evening, I didn't want to burst into flames. Oh but how sorry I felt for him, Hi! He wasn't in class this morning—big surprise—and so he was ostensibly trying to find me to tell me why. As if I wouldn't know, poor thing. I just heard them mention it on the national news! Anyway, luckily for me, we didn't really have time for a conversation. As soon as we got out of the English building, and after he stopped sobbing, his friend came and took him away."

"Well if only he'd come twenty minutes earlier. Then I could have left with you, instead of having to give that talk," reflected Hi. "But it certainly did make for a dramatic ending to my paper, wouldn't you agree?"

"Even more dramatic than you think," his sister replied. "After he and his friend began walking away from me, he turned and asked me if I thought his father had killed his mother!"

"And do you?" Hi looked down over his gold-rimmed glasses at his five-foot-four sister. He was a lofty five-foot-nine-and-a-half.

"Well, you know how the rich are, once you get them angry. I suppose he did it, yes."

"Why, Miss Musing, I find it difficult to believe that you can be so prejudiced!" declared Hi, in his best imitation of an aristocratic voice.

"And after your talk today, I find it just as hard to believe that you, Mr. Musing, cannot be proud."

They were about to continue their banter when Antigone let out a little groan. "Oh God, not the Schteks," she whispered, nodding politely to a man who had signaled to her and was approaching with his female companion.

Among the very few people Antigone knew at the party, the Schteks were the ones she would least have hoped to see. From Antigone's own department, Hans Schtek was a skinny botanist with a bad temperament and a vicious tongue. His wife was the equally boney, and even less likable, Bonnie Schtek, associate professor of English, a woman unwitting outsiders and underclassmen traditionally mistook for an angry lesbian. If she had been able to persuade her husband to attend this dinner, it was only so that they could both speak ill of it later. Antigone was wondering how to keep her brother away from such poisonous influences when the need was removed by the sound of Randall Ross's voice, pleasantly admonishing his guests to find their place tags and take their seats.

To Hi's dismay, he and Tig were seated at different tables. Antigone was fairly adept at socializing, but her brother was always very nervous in unfamiliar company, and this often led him either to babble—which frightened those interlocutors who couldn't keep up with what he said—or, alternatively, and as a way of avoiding this, to adopt a strict silence—which caused those around him to think he was either naturally morose, uncivil, or, worst of all, contemplative.

Tonight, as it turned out, Hiawatha and Antigone were each seated next to one half of a couple called the Elevenishes. Tig's companion to her right was Mr. Elevenish, an aggressively English underdean from one of the Oxbridge colleges, who was at Clare on a yearlong visiting fellowship. His had unquestionably been the best researched and most boring of all the talks that Antigone had heard. But she was polite and told him how fascinating his theories on the recurrence of Middle English cadences in the poetry of Crashaw had been. And he, in turn, was duly flattered, despite the fact that she was only a scientist.

Hi, to his left, had Mrs. Elevenish, who seemed even more English than her husband, if that were possible. The way she talked, in fact, made Hi wonder if she wasn't in actuality Lady Elevenish, or even a Her Grace; she claimed, quite loudly, to have an illustrious

ancestry going back to the left side of Charles II's bed.
And on the topic of food she was even more daunting,
which was why Hi had instantly reverted to his silent
mode.

"Ahnd you simply cahn't find gooood mutton here
in the States. I've tried for weeks on end to get some
in, but awl in vain."

It was only when she used the word "ham"—accidentally, it would seem, from her subsequent blush—
that Hi became suspicious. He was delighted to learn
from his partner on the right, a Mrs. Smith, who had
been seeing the Elevenishes for years at functions such
as this, that, in fact, Lucy Elevenish was from Texas,
loaded, but not with royal connections. Mrs. Smith dis-
burdened Hi in a whisper, and it had the happy effect
that he immediately began to participate more actively
in the conversation going on around him.

Not surprisingly, there was only one topic for discussion throughout all three groups at dinner. After
five minutes of perfunctory flattering remarks regard-
ing the success of the conference and the loveliness of
the home, everyone had something to say about the
recent discovery of Virginia Vanderlyn's body. Lucy
Elevenish was especially voluble on the topic of Virginia herself, launching immediately into a tirade that
sounded like an eighteenth-century rendition of
Chaucer:

"How well we know, that wench befoul'd her-self."[1]

As it turned out, Mistress Elevenish had no first-hand knowledge of any of the principals in the Vanderlyn tragedy. Mrs. Smith, on the other hand, had become acquainted with both Professor and Mrs. Vanderlyn while teaching on a three-year appointment in the freshman humanities program at Clare, almost two decades earlier. And so it was to her that Hi appealed for some trustworthy insight into the pair.

"Well, she was always very friendly to me. At social gatherings, I mean. A little transparent in her manners, I suppose. For example, she was always the last to arrive at a party, and it always caused a big stir. The men loved it, but the women became a little bored with the motif." Mrs. Smith, who had silver hair which she let hang down behind her head, and whose tiny, frameless glasses were no larger than her blue eyes, seemed not to include herself in either of the groups she referred to. "Of course, we weren't what you'd call intimate, just friendly acquaintances. Everything you've probably already heard about her looks was true. She had beautiful teeth, and skin, and hair. I wish I could say that she had a heart of gold, but I just don't know."

---

1. Compare this, if only for its rhythm, to the well-known opening, "Whan that Aprille with his shoures sote . . ."

"And what of Mr. Vanderlyn?" inquired Hi, hesitantly daring to sip the red wine in his glass.

"He was good-looking, too, in that way some male scholars are. You know, bookish, but also boyish. And contrary to what people say, he never seemed long-suffering. He just adored his wife."

At these last words, Hi half-expected to see Joan Fontaine walk into the room. He and Tig were planning to watch *Rebecca* on videotape, both for the thirtieth time, at some point over the coming weekend.

At Antigone's table, too, people were vying to make their beliefs about the Vanderlyns prevail. While neither of the men who flanked her could provide much information, she was lucky that the woman just beyond her male companion to the left (a sleepy older scholar who made a funny clicking noise when he chewed), was Professor Ross's wife, Laura. A nice-looking blond with an enigmatically unchanging expression, she spoke on the topic at hand with both knowledge and reserve.

"Randall and I have been friends with Cornelius for years. We came to Clare shortly after he and Virginia were married, and they were always so nice to us. Both of them."

Tig hated to sound crass and push her hostess to declare that Vanderlyn was guilty or not guilty of the horrible crime, but at the same time, she was tingling with curiosity to know the opinion of someone qualified by personal experience of the principals. She did her best to phrase her question politely.

"And do you think that Professor Vanderlyn could have done anything so brutal?"

"Love makes you do strange things, I suppose. But Cornelius a killer? Not in a million years. Virginia was the one with a temper, and she could be a bit hard, too. I've seen her snub people. There was a secretary in her husband's department whom she used to laugh at right to her face, though she refused to speak to her. She was a creature of whim, as they say." At this, Laura Ross colored slightly, perhaps thinking that she had tipped the scales too far against her erstwhile friend, Virginia. As if to make amends, she added after a pause, "But she was a kind, generous woman, who would never really have hurt a fly. I still think of her all the time, and I know I'm not the only one who misses her."

"From what I've heard, that was the root of the problem. A lot of people missed her, so to speak." This came from Mr. Elevenish, who, like his wife, had nothing but hearsay to contribute to the conversation. His comment was prompted by his increasing annoyance that the topic had shifted so quickly from the Metaphysical poets. And after he had made it, he produced an unpleasant little chuckle.

Neither Tig nor Hi were to learn much else this evening about the Vanderlyn murder, in spite of the fact that they both found their interest mounting. As they walked home from the dinner, gastronomically satisfied (although Hi had his doubts about the freshness of the mascarpone in the *tiramisu*) but intellectually piqued, they compared the little tidbits of information they had respectively obtained. It soon became clear that these amounted to almost nothing. The other guests had been either too eager and ignorant, or too reticent and far-between, to offer much of substance. They were planning to give up altogether what Hi was now calling "the case" when they arrived at Tig's cottage to find the following message on her telephone answering machine:

"Hello, my name is Cornelius Vanderlyn. Perhaps you know that I teach here at Clare in the Classics Department. I'm looking for a Miss Antigone—I mean Professor Antigone—Musing. I heard that there had been some trouble today with my son. I wonder if you could get back to me. In fact, you would do me a huge favor if you would pay me a visit at your convenience. Any time this weekend would be fine for me. I live in Ory Quad, just above the Jester's Gate. Isn't that amusing? Anyway, give me a call, at Clare 398, and we can set something up. I would be so grateful. Oh, and by all means bring

your brother, whom Mrs. Ross tells me is paying you a
visit at the present time."

And so it was in anticipation of becoming considerably more involved in the case that both Antigone
and Hiawatha drifted to sleep that night.

VIII

SURE ENOUGH, THERE WAS A JESTER, A CONCRETE copy of a stone finial at Hampton Court, in a red brick niche over the entrance to Ory Quad, where Professor Vanderlyn lived. Passing through the arch at five o'clock the following afternoon, both Hi and Tig had a good look at it, Hi noting its resemblance to Antigone's first high school boyfriend, Terence Bland.

"In fact, it could be any one of your boyfriends. You see: short, stocky, hungry, and puzzled," continued Hi.

"I hope," returned Antigone, pushing a button after the name *Vanderlyn* on a little brass plate outside of the inner gate, "I only hope you're not going to talk about my boyfriends to Professor Vanderlyn. He's got quite enough on his mind. Why did you want to come anyway?"

They were buzzed in and began their ascent to the second floor of the building, Hi answering succinctly, "To protect you, of course."

Despite her seeming peevishness, Antigone was glad her brother had come. Not to protect her—that was absurd, as Hi was a notorious coward, who invariably threw up after the tamest horror movies— but because she hated discussing her students with their parents, and Hi's empathetic support would be most welcome.

Cornelius was waiting for them at the top of the stairs. He ushered them through the outer door and into his foyer. Like the previous evening, the day was warm, so his visitors were not wearing coats, though Hi was excessively happy to remove his sports jacket and hand it to their host. Then, stepping highly and gingerly over the piles of library books that filled the little antechamber, all three walked together into the drawing room.

If Hi had been impressed with the richness of the Rosses' furnishings, the interior of Professor Vanderlyn's apartment swept him into another realm altogether. To begin with, the drawing room was enormous, probably as big as the entire ground storey of Mr. and Mrs. Ross's home. This was surprising, given the lack of space from which all colleges are known to suffer. But even more impressive than its size were the contents of the room. Perfect in itself, each surface, whether of inlaid marble or unmarred, highly polished wood, was covered with an assortment of beautiful objects. The walls, too, disappeared behind a plethora of mainly gilt-framed pictures hung from knee-level to the egg-and-dart molding high above. The overriding air of the place was that of the museum; it was a bit like being in one of the less-frequented cabinets at the Louvre. And among these mostly ancient objects and scenes, Hi and Tig found themselves feeling suddenly very young, and vaguely worried they might break something irreplaceable.

"Can I get you something to drink? I myself am just having a gin and tonic. 'Good for the liver! Good for the liver!'" Cornelius sang out in something like an imitation of a mountebank.

If Hi and Tig had known him better, they would have thought that their host was acting very oddly and out of character. As it was, they were struck by his apparent good spirits, especially given the events of the past few days. How could they know what it was like for Cornelius, still living in a strange dream, finding himself suddenly, after over a decade, dying to talk, and weirdly free to do so. He was like something, a toy or an appliance, that is wound up or plugged in after years of disuse. He jumped back to life.

Hi and Tig glanced at each other. Then Hi said, "The best gin and tonic I ever had turned out to be a martini." Cornelius seemed not to have heard, and Tig looked at Hi again. "But I'll take some fruit juice, if you have it."

"The same for me," said Antigone.

"Coming right up," said Cornelius, who disappeared behind a paneled door, to which more pictures had been bolted. Then from the kitchen, he called out, "Sit down, sit down. Make yourselves at home."

"Did he say, 'Help yourself. Take some of these things home.'?" Hi asked his sister in a whisper. "I knew I should have brought a shopping bag."

"Sshhh," warned Tig. Despite their host's invitation, neither Hi nor Tig had yet settled in a chair. They were taking a closer look at some of the details of their marvelous setting when Cornelius returned with the drinks on a tray. Hi was studying a series of little eighteenth-century gouaches of the excavations at Pompeii, and Tig was reverently perusing an enormous panorama of Knossos, the legendary city of King Minos on Crete. Cornelius put his tray down on a rare slice of empty tabletop, and then approached Antigone.

"It wasn't easy, getting everything from my old house into one big room. And even this room used to be two. I had the college knock down a wall. They were only too happy to do it, since I promised they could have some of the stuff when I die."

"And what stuff!" yodeled Hi from his place across the room.

"I'm glad it interests you. Please, feel free to take a closer look at anything you like. Handle it, even. I'm so used to these things, I hardly even see them anymore," said Cornelius, taking on a more introspective tone. While they were studying him via his possessions, he studied the brother and sister, the latter from closer up. She was lovely, he thought, truly lovely. As though she were the first woman he had seen in years. At last he stood right beside Antigone and looked at the picture with her.

"Have you been to Greece?" he inquired.

Without taking her eyes from the canvas, for it was a rich and eventful scene, accurately detailing the myriad levels and pavilions of the celebrated palace, and imaginatively filling it with innumerable tiny figures in ancient costumes, Antigone replied.

"No, but I recognize the place. It's the so-called palace of King Minos on Crete."

"That's the scientist in you, saying 'so-called'. Don't you believe, Professor Musing—may I call you Antigone? You must both call me Cornelius—that there was a King Minos, who commissioned the genius Dedalus to build him a maze, and kept the Minotaur in it?"

"Well, you're the archeologist," said Antigone. "But it seems pretty outlandish to me. Genetically speaking, I mean."

"But every life is a labyrinth," Cornelius explained softly. "And all humans are at least half beast. They've always understood that in Greece, since before the historical era." Cornelius himself marveled at hearing his own words. Not only was he experiencing a great desire to talk, he also recognized a reawakening need to teach. He had once been a great teacher; it was his true vocation. But since Virginia had gone, and his illusions of love and family life had disintegrated, he had become more and more detached, less and less involved in the occupation, becoming, like so many academics, a timeserver and even a bit of a robot.

Antigone turned to her host and took her glass from him.

"I suppose it must be fascinating, digging up the past all over the world."

"You make it sound like he writes for the tabloids," interjected Hi, walking up to them and accepting his own drink.

Cornelius smiled, eager to like the young scholars, and ever more pleased with them both. He was, from their entrance, attracted to Antigone, and so it was to her that he responded first.

"Oh, you're both every bit as fascinating as I am. And as for you, Hiawatha, all historians are glorified journalists. The only difference between them and the gossip columnist is that it's harder to sue the historian for libel. At least in this life."

After the last sentence, a hardly perceptible awkwardness cast its fleeting shadow over the three people in the room. Cornelius was most painfully aware of this, and so he immediately sat down and told them again to do likewise. Tig was next to him on the Sheraton sofa, and Hi sat opposite them on one end of a green velvet chaise.

"First of all, I wanted you to come here so that I could apologize in person for my son's behavior yesterday. I didn't know till this morning, from Randall Ross, that it was actually your talk, Hiawatha—what an unusual coincidence—that Charlie disrupted. His friend, Michael Smith, who brought Charlie to my place yesterday afternoon, never said anything about that." Cornelius stared off for a moment, then briskly began again. "Well, perhaps Michael didn't know. But I'm very sorry for the whole thing. And to you, Antigone. I wish there were some way to make it up to you both." After a second, longer pause, and like one of the Cretan athletes in the picture, Cornelius finally took the bull by the horns. "We can hardly imagine what my boy is going through right now. Well, I'm sure you've heard all about it."

Hi and Tig nodded, but seemed unable to respond. Finally, after studying his face with the same curiosity and focus she had brought to his pictures, Antigone answered Cornelius.

"Yes, we've heard a great deal, and believe me, you both have our sympathy. Of course, there's no question of apologies. Hi and I are both familiar with student problems. I only want you to know that if Charlie needs help of any kind, you must let me know."

Cornelius beamed at her, but that, too, was fleeting. "You're exactly as Charlie said. You see, I'm sure he felt badly about missing your class, because he really likes you. He's said so more than once, in so many words. And though we've never met before, you have a reputation on campus for being a wonderful teacher and well loved by the students."

"That's not surprising, given that she provides them with free beer," said Hi, chuckling. He was feeling slightly extraneous and still a bit nervous.

"How wise of you to mention alcohol. Because, of course, that was part of the problem. With Charlie, I mean. Yesterday." Cornelius moved his head forward toward Antigone. "I'm not ashamed to tell you that I'm sure he was quite drunk."

Antigone was relieved, because this confession spared her from having to divulge an identical conclusion. She was happy, as well, to defend the boy.

"But as you said, Professor Vanderlyn—I mean, Cornelius (the name seemed to Antigone as unusual as her own or her brother's, and conjured up vague images of sea captains and robber barons)—he's doubtless going through a great deal right now. I wonder if he shouldn't take the semester off."

"He won't hear of it. He told me that as soon as he arrived here. I tried to convince him that he should come away someplace with me, just to catch his breath. I'm long overdue for a sabbatical. But I can't force him. And it is, after all, his freshman year. The best I can hope for is that he'll continue to talk to me." Cornelius again adopted an intimate tone when he added, "You know, he doesn't talk to me very much. His visits are very rare, though hardly surprising yesterday. He's never been one to confide in me, since his mother left."

With the mention of Charlie's mother, Cornelius seemed to be talking to himself.

"Perhaps he blames me in some way," he continued. Then he came back with a little start. "Still, I suppose it would be more worrisome if he were to cling to me, even now," he completed his train of thought in a voice which, nevertheless, made it clear that a little more clinging would not have been unacceptable.

Hi and Tig again looked at each other. Cornelius was only too conscious of their uncertainty as to what remained to be said. So it was for their sakes that he abruptly adopted a more formal tone.

"Well, if you've forgiven us, I can only thank you again," he said, finishing off his drink. Hi and Tig took this as a cue that it was time to leave, and they were more than willing to do so. Hoping to fill the pause with physical movement, the three of them stood up, almost simultaneously. As they were leaving the luxurious room, Hi took a last backward look around.

"And thank you for having us here. I've never been in a more remarkable room. Interesting—I don't mean that in the overused sense. I mean I've never seen a room with so many beautiful proofs of so many scholarly interests." This was Hiawatha's way of saying good-bye.

Cornelius's reply marked the deliberate return to his former, perhaps colder and certainly remoter, self.

"My interests are of two varieties: those which are too private to communicate and those which are too complicated to explain. My own experiences—far-flung and expensive as they have invariably been—amount to nothing in my own mind. But," and he hesitated, as a man who cannot go through with the charade of unhappiness in the face of something that stirs in him quite the opposite emotion, "it would please me so much if you would both come back to see me again. Before you leave, Hiawatha. If only to tell me something of your own lives."

And with these words, he closed his door upon the siblings, who walked some ways toward Antigone's cottage without exchanging a word.

IX

WELL, NOW WHAT DO YOU THINK? DID HE DO IT?"
Hiawatha faced his sister like an inquisitor
across the kitchen table at her house. They were eating grilled cheese sandwiches, which Hi had made
because only he knew how. Antigone was incapable
of translating her prodigious skills with beakers and
bottles to pots and pans. Hi, on the other hand, due to
his hypochondriac streak, was a scrupulous preparer
of his own food.

Antigone's reply to her brother was long in coming, and surprisingly long when it came.

"Well, I'm beginning to entertain doubts. I mean, I
never seriously thought he did it in the first place. You

can't trust the television news to give you the real story. I did notice, when we visited him yesterday, that everything he said, after that weird, jolly way in which he opened the door, was tinged with remorse. But I've been thinking about it, and I'm sure it wasn't the remorse of a murderer. It was the remorse of a parent who thinks he's failed. When he was staring off into space, it wasn't at the dead woman. It was at the living child."

Hi was pondering this when, all of a sudden, the doorbell rang. He nearly choked. Unexpected or unanticipated callers, whether in person or on the phone, always made him lurch.

Antigone answered the door to a man who informed her immediately of his identity.

"Hello, Miss Musing. My name is Richard Staves. I am the chief of police here in Westerly. May I come in?"

Antigone was mystified, but led the detective to the kitchen, where her brother was now standing, though he was still chewing his sandwich. Hi extended his hand as Antigone introduced the two men to each other.

"Please sit down," Antigone gestured to a chair. "Can I get you something to drink? Maybe some coffee?"

"That would be excellent, yes. Thank you," replied Staves.

The three of them sat down, Hiawatha gazing widely at his sister, who was pouring the coffee from a ceramic pot.

The police chief, who seemed very natural and at his ease, took a sip and then began.

"I'm very sorry to bother you, Miss Musing. Especially while your brother is visiting. But as you know, a very dramatic thing happened here in our little town a few days ago. The body of a woman was found at the Vanderlyn house. The house, that is, formerly belonging to Professor Cornelius Vanderlyn, whom I think you know."

Detective Staves stopped and took another slow sip of coffee. As he did so, he looked from the brother to the sister without speaking. His penetrating but unthreatening eyes were light blue, and he had that shadow of a beard which some men acquire by noon whether or not they shave in the morning. He swallowed and then went on.

"Well, identifying the body was easy enough. It was Virginia Scott Vanderlyn, wife of the professor. And our preliminary lab reports make it quite clear that she was buried alive. Before death, she suffered a severe blow to the back of her head, from the wooden post that was buried next to her. It's possible that the person who hit her thought she was dead, but death didn't occur till many hours later."

Despite seeming relaxed, Staves recited this information swiftly and as though eager to get such details out of the way. Then he spoke more slowly.

"I'm sorry to bring you such news on a beautiful Sunday afternoon, but there is a reason I'm telling you both this. You see, the police know that you went to see Professor Vanderlyn last night."

Hi's mouth dropped open, and Antigone went pale. They felt suddenly as though they had been transported into an old episode of *Perry Mason*, a show of which Hi was extremely fond.

"Yes, we did," Antigone responded calmly, though it was costing her some effort. "It was about his son, Charlie. Charlie is my student in Chemistry 101. My brother, Hiawatha, was giving a talk at a conference, and the poor kid turned up there, looking for me."

Detective Staves smiled. "Yes, we know that, too." Then he winked at Hiawatha, who slowly put down his own drink, as though gathering together his energy, before bursting out.

"Good heavens! Have you been following us?"

"No, not you. But we have been keeping an eye on the Vanderlyns. And you've both intersected with them several times in the past few days. We couldn't help but notice." Detective Staves managed to look both sheepish and sure of himself as he took another sip of his coffee.

"I doubt if my sister can help you in any way," said Hi, suspiciously. "You must already know everything there is to know, including what we had for dinner last night and what we watched on television before we went to bed."

Detective Staves laughed.

Both Hiawatha and Antigone looked confused, the shared emotion bringing out a family resemblance which was not always obvious.

Finally Chief Staves resumed.

"No, listen. You're not supposed to be suspicious of our methods. You're supposed to be impressed by our results. And that's why I'm here. To ask you a favor. You see, aside from the obvious bizarre circumstances, there are a number of inconsistencies in this case, and frankly, I'm not one of those television cops who wants to do everything all by himself. I figure as long as I survive the case and get the bulk of the credit, I'm happy for any help I can get."

Antigone listened with quiet interest to what Staves was saying. She didn't yet believe in his bonhomie, while Hi was even less credulous. Still, she spoke up.

"But, like my brother said, I don't think we know anything more than the stories and rumors we've heard. How can we help?"

"Well, for one thing, I thought you might talk to the kid, Charlie Vanderlyn. As you just said, he deserves some sympathy, and I don't want a lot of cops hounding him. More to the point, I don't want a lawsuit against the police for harassing some poor kid whose mother was just dug up after being buried in their basement. So I asked President Trowbridge if there was a counselor or somebody here at school he might feel comfortable talking to, at least to begin with. Trowbridge called Professor Vanderlyn himself, and Professor Vanderlyn suggested you. You see, it's all aboveboard. The father understands our predicament. And apparently the kid likes you and trusts you. He must, because he came looking for you the other day."

Both Hiawatha and the police chief gazed at Antigone, who was thoughtful for a moment before speaking.

"Yes, but what do you want me to talk to him about? I can't just walk up to him after class and say 'You did well on your quiz. Now what do you think about the murder of your mother?'"

Staves smiled again—it turns out that this was his natural expression—and then replied.

"No, no. All we want you to do is to ask him if there's anything on his mind, anything he'd like to talk about, perhaps something he remembers about his mother that might help the police. You can be very honest. It's all aboveboard," the policeman repeated. "And it's really in his best interests to tell somebody."

"But he was only a little kid when his mother left
. . . I mean, died," interjected Hi, whose curiosity was
continuing to get the best of him.

"Eight years old is old enough to notice things,"
said Staves. "Besides, the story didn't end ten years
ago. It only just began. He's a big boy now."

"And of course, he might have something to say
about his father." Antigone's tone was sad and a little cool.

"Well, of course, there is that possibility. But what
the boy has to say might help his father, too. We
haven't drawn any conclusions yet."

Once again Hiawatha and Antigone looked at
each other, this time for some indication as to what
Antigone should do. Detective Staves gave them a
moment before spelling out the alternatives.

"You must believe me when I say that I'm thinking of the boy. If you won't talk to him, we'll just have
to wait until we can get a police psychiatrist to talk to
him, and believe me, that's not much better than the
high beam in the bunker."

Antigone tried hard to read Hiawatha's mind,
then she nodded. "I'll do it," she said, "but only in the
interest of unbiased justice and for my student's
sake." She was going to say more, when Hi sprang
from his seat and interrupted her.

"Yes, my sister will help you, but on one or two
conditions. First, you tell us—in confidence, of

course—everything about the case so far. Not the secret stuff, but the stuff that the news people keep hinting at or misreporting."

Detective Staves smiled, but this time it was in surprise.

"Well, I'm not sure . . ."

Hi continued without letting him speak.

"And second, you arrange for us to visit the Vanderlyn house. Call it curiosity, but we want to see the scene of the crime. Those are our—I mean, my sister's—conditions."

Staves frowned. He loved to bargain with reasonable people, and he knew he would be getting a pretty good deal. "As far as seeing the house, I don't see why you want to, but I don't see why you couldn't. My men have been all over it with microscopes. And as for what we know, aside from anything secret, as you put it, I'd be happy to tell you what I can. As I said, I'm a guy who loves assistance. Anything that gets me home earlier."

Hi resumed his seat and Antigone drew hers in closer to the table, the latter casting the former yet another puzzled look before saying aloud, "And I thought I was reading your mind."

Detective Staves, rising and pouring himself a second cup of coffee from the pot on the stove, then proceeded to outline for them the basic facts of what was now truly their case. His voice was even, his style of narrative plain but precise.

"On October 11, 1989, Virginia Vanderlyn, aged thirty-six, wrote a letter to her husband, indicating her intention to leave him. Then she disappeared. She was not seen by anybody—at least not by anybody that we've found so far—after the morning of that day. But nobody doubted that she had simply gone away, and most people assumed she had run off with some man. She was considered by many people promiscuous, and this would explain her use of the first person plural in her letter."

Staves interrupted his narrative to remove from his briefcase—a worn and clearly ancient leather bag with a broken clasp—a photocopy of Virginia's letter, which it was convenient for him to have at hand. This he passed to Hi and Tig, who studied it together.

Then Staves went on.

"Anyway, as I said, Mrs. Vanderlyn disappeared, leaving behind a husband, Professor Cornelius Vanderlyn, and an eight-year-old son, named Charlie. By all accounts, Professor Vanderlyn was very upset by this turn of events. Within weeks of his wife's disappearance, he moved himself and his child out of the house and into the apartment he now occupies at the college. Less than a year after his mother vanished, Charlie received what appeared to be a birthday card from her, enclosing a small sum of money. He received the same thing every year at his birthday and at

Christmas, each card signed simply, "Your Mum." These were postmarked from a variety of places: New York, Chicago, and even from big cities in Europe. Charlie, subsequently, went away to school. Cornelius stayed at Clare and continued his teaching. Everything seemed relatively normal until the college decided to renovate the old mansion for use as some sort of alumni clubhouse. Last Thursday afternoon, a team of construction workers engaged in excavating the house's rotting foundation turned up the body—the skeletal remains—of Mrs. Vanderlyn. She was found in the northwest corner of the basement, under a pile of wooden debris and about four feet of earth."

"Who was the last person to see her alive?" Hi couldn't wait to ask.

"And what was she wearing?" asked Tig.

Staves was again pleasantly surprised.

"I guess there is something to this education thing, after all. Well, the last person to see her alive was the head of the school's engineering services, a big guy named Chuck Vigevano, who came to measure her old boiler first thing in the morning of the day she disappeared. He used to do a lot of jobs for the Vanderlyns, even though the house had nothing to do with the college at that time. And like all the men I've interviewed so far in connection with this case, he was very fond of Mrs. Vanderlyn and made no bones about saying so.

"As to what she was wearing, I'm glad you asked. She was fully dressed, in a skirt and blouse. On what was left of the blouse we found a little gold and diamond pin. It was this pin that Professor Vanderlyn recognized when we were removing the body. But curiously, there was no trace of her wedding ring, which Vanderlyn insists he has never seen since she left, and all of her friends—she had a few, such as the librarian, Hermione Pole, and a former student, Paul Mullaney, whom we've contacted in New York—claim she always wore, though that strikes me as a bit ironic. I mean, if a robber had gotten into the house, he would have taken the pin and the ring, but if he were only going to take one of the two, the ring would be less valuable and more incriminating, if you see what I mean."

Hi was rapt with attention, Antigone a little less obviously, but just as intensely so. Both were making mental notes, especially with regard to the names that Staves mentioned. Hi wanted to push him for more of these.

"I'm sorry," the detective replied, "I've told you everything I can. It would lose me my job if I started listing all the men with whom Mrs. Vanderlyn was said to have shared something wonderful. Some of them her husband's colleagues, too."

Hi and Tig, though still relatively new to academia, were nevertheless not so naive as to be shocked by the notion of intra- or extra-departmental adultery. With regard to specifics, they could do their own investigation. But when, after finishing his coffee, Staves rose to leave, it looked as though Hi was going to block his way.

"And about our visiting the Vanderlyn house? You'll arrange that?"

"Go anytime you like. Today if you want to. It's so nice out. And tell the officer there that I said it's all right. But there's nothing to see." Then the policeman focused on Antigone. "And as for you, Professor Musing, thank you for your help. We'll be in touch about your student. The sooner the better, I think you'd agree." With that, he headed for the door.

When the three of them were standing together in the entryway, he offered them his card, with a final remark.

"By the way, you had steak and mashed potatoes. And you, Mr. Musing, didn't eat your peas. Then you watched a videotape of Alfred Hitchcock's *Rebecca*, a perfect choice, I thought." Detective Staves smiled broadly, then turned from the house, adding in a cheerful tone, "Good-bye, and thank you again."

Hiawatha closed the door with a gasp, unable to articulate beyond that his reaction to the unfailing audacity of the outside world.

X

HIAWATHA WAS WALKING FASTER THAN HIS SISTER, so every few steps he had to wait for her to catch up. The two of them were nevertheless carrying on a lively conversation.

"No, I've thought about what we were saying before Detective Staves arrived, and I'm sure Cornelius isn't the killer. Laura Ross, who knows him pretty well, laughed at the idea. At least, she would have laughed if she were the kind of person who laughed. But it was just as clear that Mr. Staves thinks he's guilty. Hi, would you please stop running ahead? You're making me feel like a dog out for a walk with its impatient owner."

"Well if you wouldn't stop at every lamppost, the simile wouldn't ring so true."

Antigone giggled, but by no means increased her pace. She was vaguely looking in shop windows, most of which were dark since it was Sunday afternoon. She couldn't at all understand her brother's anxiety to see inside the Vanderlyn house, which was where they were going, Hi now several steps ahead again, pretending to tug her along on an invisible leash. Despite her own meandering gait and her brother's energetic leaping about, both were seriously considering the situation in which they now found themselves, though their interests in it were different, and they confronted it in very different ways.

Antigone treated the problem according to her academic training, that is, scientifically. And she treated her own attitude with the same professional scrutiny. To begin with, she duly noted her unrepressed feeling of uncertainty with regard to the talk she had promised to have with Charlie Vanderlyn. Then she added up everything she had been told about that famous family and separated it in her mind from what was provable fact. She measured the little evidence she had, tried to speculate as to the far greater quantity of information she was still lacking, and experimented with possibilities in her mind. As yet, the only conclusion she could risk was that Cornelius was innocent, but her reason for thinking him so, she had to admit to herself, was that she had liked him and found him eminently human and sympathetic at their first meeting.

All of this represented a slower but more reliable process of inquiry than Hiawatha's. He saw the mystery not so much as a thing to be solved, as something to throw himself into. For Antigone, it was a kind of intellectual task, like her own research, and nothing could be more enjoyable for her. But for Hiawatha, it was the antithesis of his research and the other daily tasks which made up his life. It was something to get lost in, other people's lives, and passions of the sort he had previously only read about in books.

Now is perhaps the moment to make an important observation concerning Hiawatha, namely that he was, unlike his sister, recurrently if not consistently discontent with his lot. As a result, he came to personify two seemingly contradictory states, the state of being overbooked or harried, and that of being bored. Complicating the matter, Hi was also plagued with a perennial feeling that everything around him was finite, already known and measured, and clearly this story of the Vanderlyns contradicted that. He didn't care who was guilty, but he cared that they didn't know. The fact was, ever since he was a boy, Hiawatha had tended regularly to worry that what was good or worthy of interest—in his own life or in the history of the world—formed a supply of experiences and sensations that had by this time already been all but depleted. Consequently, he was often struck by the unappealing notion that he must be living in an aftermath, an era of making do. In happier moods, however, he was struck by the inverse possibility, that, speaking for himself, after his difficult teens (the happiest years of his life were his early childhood)—as, speaking globally, after the development of the hydrogen bomb—everything was extra, that he and the world were no longer cornered, but living, now, on the other side of the walls, and that all of this was, in a way, a bonus, superfluous, more than was expected or deserved. This latter, more optimistic but no doubt equally unnatural, way of thinking nevertheless brought Hiawatha great pleasure, a sense of exhilaration and immunity such as ghosts perhaps feel; it was also, paradoxically but in any case, the closest he could come to approximating calm.

So the two siblings were very much together and just as much apart when they paused in front of the Vanderlyn gate. The wind, which had been on the rise since morning, whipped the dead leaves along the drive in miniature cyclones that dissolved in a moment. It was definitely becoming colder.

"Excuse me," called out Hiawatha, to a dimly silhouetted figure seated just inside the glass-paned front door of the house. Hi signaled broadly with both arms, and the figure rose and came out onto the porch.

"What is it you want?" shouted the figure, who was an older man in a plaid flannel shirt and dark corduroy trousers.

"We've been sent by Police Chief Staves. He wanted us to have a look around the house," Hiawatha explained to the man, who was making his way quickly down the twenty steep yards of the driveway toward the pair.

Antigone winced at, but could not altogether help admiring, the way her brother, with a slight twist of the truth, made it sound as though they were working for the police. Maybe in Hi's mind, they were.

"Oh yes, I got a call a short while ago. You're the two teachers," said the genial man, with his neat grey hair and his wiry figure, as he unlocked the gate. He looked to be at least seventy, but an energetic and engaging seventy.

"Professors," said Hi, who could, on occasion, be pompous.

"And who are you?" asked Antigone, who was hoping for a brief visit and saw no reason why it should not be a pleasant one, as well.

"I'm nobody now. I WAS Sergeant Bayliss of the Westerly Police. Now I'm retired, and every once in a while, they call me when they need a babysitter for a crime scene. So here I sit, reading and thinking in a big spooky house, for eight hours at a time." Though the ex-sergeant was ostensibly bewailing his fate, both Tig and Hi could see that he seemed pleased to be doing something. Probably a widower, they thought simultaneously, following him through the rusty gate.

Both Hi and Tig took a moment to size up the house before following Sergeant Bayliss in. It certainly deserved the mansion epithet, for its proportions were very grand and immediately put Hi in mind of the Schuyler homestead in Albany, New York, which must have been built at about the same time. What had originally been the substantial, square, three-storey facade was now partially obscured by a number of later architectural excrescences. The largest of these, the long porch or veranda, had not marred the symmetry of the front, but the extension of the western side of the house, and the addition of numerous, oddly spaced bow windows, and even a little octagonal turret on the second floor, certainly had. What remained was nevertheless still appealing to the eye, a grand palimpsest of a residence, two centuries in the making.

In the front hall, which was twice as wide as most colonial American entryways, Hi and Tig paused again. Sergeant Bayliss told them that Staves had

made him promise to accompany the "curious pair"—
that's what Chief Staves had called them—on their
tour. He also informed them, in a very friendly voice,
that they were not to touch anything nor to wander
off on their own.

"It's just like visiting a house museum," muttered
Hi as they waited for the sergeant to retrieve a flashlight from the kitchen. The electricity, other than that
wired in especially for the construction workers and
the police, had long been turned off, and much of the
house was dark.

When Bayliss returned, they followed him from
room to room on the ground floor. As the police chief
had promised, there was very little to see. The rooms
were, for the most part, empty of furnishings, and it
was difficult to tell, from the water-stained wallpaper
and the wooden paneling with its dirty paint, which
rooms had been which. That the house had once
been a showplace was very clear. There were elegant,
marble-framed fireplaces throughout, and in the four
great rooms they had seen so far, the ceilings were
beautifully plastered with elaborate medallions or, in
the case of one room, slightly coved and embossed
with an intricate pattern of roses and vines.

When they had finished with the downstairs, the
three of them made their way slowly up, past the
enormous Palladian aperture on the landing, to the

second floor. Occasionally, Sergeant Bayliss would offer a remark, such as "They don't build them like this anymore," and once, surprisingly, "All this for one family! Now you can see why people have revolutions." He winked, and Hi and Tig smiled, not unsympathetically.

They continued their walk through what were more confidently to be identified as the bedrooms. It was in the second of these that Antigone felt she was sure they had found Virginia's room, not the bedroom she shared with her husband, but a room which was her own.

"But how can you tell?" queried Hi.

"Look," she insisted. "The wallpaper, which seems comparatively new, is very feminine. The whole room still smells a bit like perfume." All three of them sniffed a little, taking in the combined odors of must, lavender, and patchouli, and Antigone continued. "Not the sort I like, but it's still feminine. They certainly wouldn't have kept a little boy in here. And the room opens onto both the bathroom and the biggest room, which must have been their bedroom."

"If you say so," said Hi.

Antigone felt quite certain. She had been reluctant to come to the house, but now that she had, she found herself enthusiastically looking for tangible evidence, not of the crime (anything possibly connected with the murder had obviously already been removed), but of the individuals who had lived there. Hi, on the other hand, was there to indulge his instincts and to acquire some sense of the atmosphere in which these people had lived and loved, fought and, fatally perhaps, betrayed. So even in silence, Hi and Tig were working together. Theirs was an unconscious joining of the enlightened and romantic ways of seeing; the alliance was one that had never failed to benefit them both, curbing, as it did, Antigone's slight cynicism and Hiawatha's tendency toward melodrama.

On the third floor, which Hi had insisted was included in Detective Staves's promise that they were to be shown "the whole house," somewhat more was to be seen than on the two floors below. This, the attic area, had probably been intended for storage when the house was built. It had subsequently been expanded, both upward and outward, and dormer windows had been added at the back. At some point, and in keeping with eighteenth- and nineteenth-century customs, it had been used as a nursery, joined as it was to a series of low-ceilinged bedrooms. A few bits of furniture remained from that indeterminate period, and among these was a little hand-pegged, three-shelf bookcase, which looked like the diminutive exercise of a very young, or very unpromising, apprentice. Hi and Tig bent down to look at it, and sure enough, near the base, they found the signature of the boy who had made it: "Cornelius J. Vanderlyn, aged 9 years and 3 months."

"You see," said Antigone. "I told you he didn't do it. The person who bungled that darling little bookcase never buried his wife alive."

It should no longer strike the reader as odd that Hiawatha agreed completely with his sister on this point. Sergeant Bayliss, who was listening, laughed out loud, but when they questioned him as to why, he said simply, "No, no, I think you could be right."

Only one area of the house remained to be seen, and that was the cellar or basement, where the body had been found.

"Are you sure you want to go down there?" asked the old policeman. He seemed to be speaking from fatigue more than anything else.

Antigone would have been happy to forego a visit to that particular spot, but Hi was adamant.

"I was only thinking that the sergeant is getting a bit tired," Antigone appealed to her brother's human side.

Hi thought for a moment before speaking.

"Look, I think you should just stay up here and rest. My sister and I" (for Hi had no intention of going down alone) "will just pop down for two minutes with the flashlight. You can just wait at the door. I promise we won't be more than two minutes."

Sergeant Bayliss said that wouldn't be possible, that he had promised Detective Staves he would accompany them, and that he didn't mind at all. So the three of them, with Hi in the lead, solemnly descended the kitchen stairs to the scene of the actual crime.

Below, it was pitch black. Hi asked to carry the flashlight, as he was going first. He made sure that he never lost physical contact with his sister, as they followed the spotlight he was casting into and through a series of wide, subterranean spaces, complete with all the cobwebs and creaking floorboards from the horror films they had seen. The air was cool and damp and brought back to both Hiawatha and Antigone memories of the catacombs they had visited together in Rome. There were, at irregular intervals, odd chinks in the unfinished wood of the walls, which allowed little breezes or drafts of chilled air to sift between the uncertain spaces, bearing with them hardly perceptible gradations of grey shadow. At last, at the direction of Sergeant Bayliss, Hi turned the light on what they immediately recognized was the yellow tape with which the police had marked the site of the recent excavation, its bright color sounding a strange note of mirth, like a festive streamer, against the otherwise unmitigated drabness of the setting.

All three paused over the scar in the floor, which extended several feet into the earth, where the body had been found. Hi was about to speak when suddenly there was an odd whirring noise, followed by something coming at them from above. Hi dropped the flashlight, and brother and sister let out a yell identical in all but pitch.

"What in the hell?" screeched Hi, groping frantically and automatically for his sister's hand.

Sergeant Bayliss lit a match and recovered the flashlight, which had gone out when Hi dropped it. When he had turned it on again, he let out a broad chuckle. Hi and Tig remained speechless.

"A bat," Sergeant Bayliss informed them merrily.

"Yuck," said Hi, but Tig was now laughing, too.

"Don't worry," she explained. "I recently read that only fifteen percent of them carry rabies."

"And the other eighty-five percent are vampires," countered Hi with disgust. "Let's get the heck out of this place."

And so, with Sergeant Bayliss thanking them heartily for an amusing afternoon, Hiawatha and Antigone returned with him to the gate, both still feeling a bit shaky, and Hi unable to erase from his mind the sensation that there was something furry, and possibly fanged, nestling at the base of his spine.

XI

CORNELIUS VANDERLYN COULD NOT SIT STILL. HE paced inside his apartment like an animal in a cage. A very expensively decorated cage, as we have seen. But today, all the priceless details of his surroundings only added to Professor Vanderlyn's feeling of suffocation. He would have liked to strip the walls, clear the floor and the furniture of their rugs and trinkets, and start a great bonfire in the center of the room. *But,* he remembered with a pensive smile, *I've promised half of it to the college.* So instead, he decided to go for a walk.

The day, while still bright, was getting distinctly cooler. He had no idea exactly where he was going, since he hadn't just walked out like this for some time, perhaps since his own undergraduate years, spent in the same town. At first, his feet seemed determined to bring him to the library; he had to make a deliberate effort to break with that routine, finally striking out toward the more spacious residential properties and the area around Westerly's sole commercial avenue, St. Romuald Street. This long, S-shaped thoroughfare, lined with shops appealing either to the student occupants of the town—who were invariably short of cash—or the genteel faculty and administrative functionaries of the college—with their love of gourmet foods and English gewgaws—was also known as the parade, an allusion to the fact that during the Revolution, it had witnessed alternating military processions of patriots and defenders of the Crown.

At first, it struck Cornelius as odd that the parade was so deserted, the shops so dark. But then he remembered that it was Sunday. He tried to think of someplace that might be open, if only to distract himself with the problem of achieving a specific goal, and lighted on the possibility of the Colonial Ladies' Bookstore. This was a used-book shop that Cornelius had frequented in his childhood, one of a type of establishment which is quintessential to an east-coast college town and acts as a sort of stamp of authenticity for natives and outsiders alike. The Colonial

Ladies were a charitable organization made up of local women who purveyed old volumes for cash, which they subsequently used to fund projects such as the purchase of notable antiques for the Westerly Museum. As he headed off, he couldn't help but smile, remembering the volunteers who had run the shop in his youth, women with names like "Malvina" and "Libby," who reeked of sachet and snapped back and forth at each other and the customers without ever actually starting a fistfight. If they had, he recalled, there was one woman in particular who could have beaten them all; she was a heavyset lady with a bust like an outcropping of rock and a head like Gertrude Stein's, complete with the mustache and pince-nez.

Cornelius turned down a little side street off the parade, and was delighted to find that, not only was the shop still there, it was still open on a Sunday afternoon. He stepped in and found, immediately inside to the left of the door, a familiar profile, though he had not known it for long. It was Antigone Musing, and she was engrossed in a small book that he recognized as one he had written himself.

"Well, I approve of your reading list, if this is what you require," Cornelius began, softly so as not to startle her nor bring down the wrath of the Colonial Ladies.

Nevertheless, Antigone jumped.

"Goodness," she said in a loud whisper. "That's the second time today." And then she blushed.

"Second time for what?" inquired Cornelius, coming nearer.

"Second time I've been taken by surprise," explained Antigone. She was reluctant to describe the first time, because it would be rather awkward to explain that she had just come from a police tour of this man's former home. But she certainly preferred Cornelius to the bat. Fortunately for Tig, Hi had come upon them, too, with his arms full of heavy old hardcovers, some in their original wrappers.

"Hello," said Hi to Vanderlyn, a little distantly. "What a coincidence."

"I was just out taking a walk," said Cornelius with perfect equanimity and friendliness.

"So were we," said Antigone, and then, to avoid more detailed questions as to what she and her brother had been doing this afternoon, she turned abruptly to Hi.

"What are you doing with all those books? We can't carry them all back. You're sweating as it is, and I'm ready for a nap."

"No, I couldn't afford them, anyway. But I wanted you to see what treasures those old hags have been hoarding."

Cornelius deduced, from the way in which Hiawatha referred to the Colonial Ladies, that he had already had a run-in with one of them. In this, he was correct. Nevertheless, Hi was kneeling down on the thinly-carpeted floor and unloading his books like a merchant in the desert. With childish enthusiasm he held up and gave a little background on each of the works he coveted.

"And just look! A second edition of Ruskin's *Stones of Venice* for twelve dollars! All the plates still accounted for. 'From the library of Elspeth Henley,'" Hi read the bookplate. "Well, Miss Henley, whoever you are, we thank you." Then he turned to his sister, and reached out to see what she had been reading. Antigone allowed him to look, blushing again.

"*The Body and the Temple: Greek Art of the Archaic Period*," Hi read aloud, his interest rising with his voice, "By Cornelius Vanderlyn the second! Well, well, this truly is a coincidence."

Cornelius was intrigued by the interplay between the brother and sister. He was also secretly flattered by Antigone's apparent interest in himself, and, less consciously but more deeply, by her change of color.

"That's my first book," he spoke objectively, though he would have preferred to make a joke. But the work had a special meaning for him, not only because it had been his first, but also because he had dedicated it to his wife. So there she was again, appearing where he least expected her, as she had done innumerable times since their marriage, and even as an apparition after her disappearance. But now she was dead. The thought caught up with him and might have brought him down, but he resisted it.

"And what, pray tell, is it like to come upon a book you've written in a used-book shop?"

Hi had not meant to be unkind when he asked this question. In fact, Tig knew, her brother would be genuinely awed by such a circumstance, and his curiosity would be a form of praise in his own mind. But she also knew that Professor Vanderlyn might not see it that way, and she had a sudden desire to shield him from offense.

"Hi, please. You're being nosey."

"I am not. Or maybe I am, but I don't think it's bad." Hi was a bit miffed. And he sensed, for the first time, his sister's awakening interest in Vanderlyn beyond the story of the murder. He found that this irritated him slightly, but he said nothing more.

"Oh, your brother is right," Cornelius intervened. "I'm not saying that he's nosey, but I agree with him that being nosey isn't really all bad. For instance, nowadays, in this country, you want to know who your neighbors are."

When he said this, both Antigone and Hiawatha at last found themselves face to face with something they had both been groping around since they had met Cornelius a few days before. In short, this man, for all his sophistication and obvious intellectual power, his wisdom and his eloquence, was completely incapable of entertaining the thought that he might be suspected of his wife's murder. For Antigone, this realization was the final confirmation of his innocence; for Hi, it was at least a strong argument in the same direction.

Antigone decided to turn the conversation back to books, the topic least threatening to anyone present, and so she began by praising what she had been perusing.

"I myself am very impressed by how beautifully you write. Though I'm not, of course, qualified to comment on your scholarship, I trust it implicitly because of your powers of description and the logical way in which you draw your conclusions. Take this passage, for example . . ." and here Antigone raised the book slightly, and quoted a sentence aloud.

"'One way in which we can translate the function of the *kouros*, or Greek youth, into our own post-Christian way of thinking is to realize that, in its nudity and the impression it gives of being new-born—the awkwardness and stiffness which are the universal conditions of re-awakening—it is the naked body of the dead brought back, resurrected and perfected for eternity in stone.' Well," Antigone went on, "I don't know anything about Greek art, but I am moved by your desire that I should be able to see it in my own terms."

"Sounds awfully racy to me," said Hiawatha, scratching the back of his neck and avoiding his sister's eyes. "Anyway, you can't really explain art or translate it. It's like the past, intangible, and thank God, too."

Cornelius smiled again. Choosing to focus not on the young woman's praise, nor on the young man's sarcasm, but rather on the ignorance which Antigone and, by implication, her brother seemed to acknowledge with regard to the topic of ancient culture, he addressed them both.

"You sound as though you think art is an illusion. Is that what you were taught? Something inaccessible, something unreal? Not at all. The easiest proof is architecture, especially the architecture of the ancients. You think the first temple of Hera at Paestum is an illusion? Hardly. It's very real, very big, very heavy. You can't mess with it; a single drum from one of its columns could crush all three of us at once. That's the real problem. That's where the anxiety about the illusion comes from. Despite reformations and restorations, Leonardo's *Last Supper* still survives.

Compared to art, we're the short-lived, the insecure, the illusory ones."

Cornelius, when he made this little speech, impressed both members of his audience. Tig, in fact, felt strangely moved. At the same time, with his ardent belief in the power of art, Cornelius had also struck a nerve in Antigone, though it was one well beneath the surface. As a child at home, her parents had drilled into her a respect for all forms of art, for which she was naturally grateful. Her mother had done this quietly, and so more convincingly, by taking her and her siblings on numerous trips to concerts and museums in and around Boston. Her father, on the other hand, had often seemed in the throes of an angry determination that all his children should develop a veneration for the intangible things, which, if he was any proof of their effect, only brought bitterness and a sense of unfulfilled longing. And so Antigone, and Hiawatha too, for that matter, sensed a split in their relationship with the higher things, painting and literature and music. For Hiawatha, this created a discord which colored both his inner and outer being; one sensed the conflict the minute one met him. But Antigone, a scientist by nature and choice, seemed to have no problem resolving this split. She loved art, she loved her parents, she was—to use a metaphor that would have pleased and puzzled her—as clear as the circle of light at the top of the Pantheon, casting a ray of tolerance over all. But deep down, well out of reach of her consciousness, a sad and lingering distrust of all things intangible remained. It was this that Cornelius unintentionally stirred when he spoke.

Hiawatha, after a respectful pause, admitted to suddenly feeling very hungry. In fact, he was anxious to be away from Cornelius Vanderlyn, if only to collect his own thoughts and to sort out his impressions of both the house they had just been visiting and its former occupant. He was also eager to get his sister alone and to voice his suspicions that she was falling for this man. The idea of his younger sister being in love was not a problem for Hi, who genuinely wanted her to be happy. But he worried at the appropriateness of the possible object of her interest; they should at least make certain of Cornelius's innocence before letting him get any closer. So Hi, hastily and haphazardly re-shelving the books he had decided not to buy, persuaded his sister that it was time they should be going. And then, Hi impatiently and Antigone less willingly, they said good-bye to Cornelius, who frowned at the irony of being left with his own open book in his hand.

XII

A NTIGONE GATHERED UP HER NOTES FROM THE
lectern, and stuffed them into her briefcase.
She was not customarily sloppy, but today she was
distracted. This morning, prior to giving her lecture,
she had seen Charlie Vanderlyn and his friend, that
same Michael Smith who had rescued him from her
the other day, outside of the classroom. Initially, she
hadn't been able to tell them apart. This was not the
first time she had experienced the strange apprehen-
sion that all of her students were beginning to look
alike, or at least familially related. Row after row in the
lecture hall they sat, both the boys and the girls, their
loose-hanging denim jeans revealing their colored

boxer shorts, and their long, usually uncombed hair flanking their wide, for the most part intelligent, eyes. They were distinguishable only with regard to the number and location of their piercings. Antigone hoped that this phenomenon was more a sign of the quickly changing times, than one that she was growing old, or her eyes weaker.

At any rate, she had approached and greeted both young men, before turning to Charlie and asking him if he wouldn't mind staying a few minutes after class today to talk with her. The boy, now as sober and alert as ever, seemed to have been expecting such a request. Without the slightest indication of shyness, or even awareness that he had caused her embarrassment the previous week, he smiled and agreed. And so, after a lecture which she could not consider among her best, she walked up into the second row of desks in the small science amphitheater and sat in the one next to Charlie, who was placidly waiting there.

"I feel so sorry about what happened last week, Charlie, and I wanted to repeat that if you need anyone to talk to . . ."

As though only waiting for an opportunity, Charlie interrupted her.

"No, Professor Musing. I'm the one who's sorry. I'm only thankful I can't remember everything that happened." He looked at her a little archly, and then went on. "And please tell your brother I'm sorry. At least, my father said that the guy I barged in on was your brother."

"Yes," answered Antigone vaguely, "that was my brother, Hiawatha, and he's already forgiven you. But I didn't ask you to stay after just to talk about the incident at the English conference. I wanted to ask you if there's anything you wanted to say, to me, about anything, about your father or mother or anything at all." She paused, shrinking inside. She felt she had no way—and no will—to enter into this discussion. It was like going back down into the Vanderlyn basement, without a light.

Charlie was thoughtful for a moment, and it was impossible for Antigone to interpret the pause. Finally, he looked straight into her eyes.

"Are you talking about what I said before we left you the other day? About my father being a suspect? I was just upset. And I wasn't feeling well, either."

"You get along well with your father, don't you?" ventured Antigone.

"We have our ups and downs." Charlie's tone was becoming slightly harder, but again, Antigone couldn't be sure this was defensiveness, or simply a way of remaining calm in the face of what must, for him, be an unbearably painful subject. And if it was defensiveness, what was he defending? His privacy? His mother or his father or both? Antigone wished he would say something, anything, that she could pass on to that policeman as a clear proof that the Vanderlyns were a family like any other, with the one minor exception that the mother had been buried in the cellar. By a complete stranger.

"Well, Charlie, as I say, if you do ever need to talk about all this . . . I mean, I can only imagine how difficult it must be . . ."

"Can you?" Charlie interrupted her again, but his tone was not the least bit rude. The longer they sat together, under a cloud of unspoken and uncertain emotions, the more it seemed as though he might have something to say. At last he continued.

"Oh Professor Musing, my father's not a bad man at all. Just a little old-fashioned. I know what people are saying about him. It's worse than what they say about my mother." Charlie's lip trembled, as the innocent child emerged from the depths of the maturing young man. Antigone decided it was too late to turn back.

"So you love and trust your father. That's what I was hoping you'd say. But Charlie, there are people— the police, for instance—who think that you might know something that will help you and your father to get to the bottom of this terrible situation." Antigone winced again, but went on. "Is there, Charlie, anything you can think of, anything you remember, even from years ago, that might help your father and the police to find out the truth?"

"Why are you asking me?" said Charlie with sudden harshness.

"Well, I believe your father himself wanted me to talk to you. To listen to you more than to talk." Saying this, she felt another wave of awkwardness, recalling that Cornelius himself had said nothing to her about her being enlisted to speak to his son, though he had an opportunity at the bookstore when they had bumped into each other yesterday. Not that she and Hi had given him much time before leaving him there. Still, it was hardly likely that Staves had lied to her about Professor Vanderlyn's authorization of this discussion.

"That's the real problem!" Charlie shouted abruptly, bringing his fist down onto his desk. "Everybody's always helping my father, feeling sorry for him. The Hugheses, and that horrible lady, Judy Dumont! Hanging around. Pitying. What about my mother? Did anybody think to help or pity her? She's the one who was murdered, and all of them hated her! Disgusting intellectual hypocrites!" Charlie was shaking, but he did not, to Antigone's surprise and relief, start to cry. Nevertheless, his voice became painfully hushed when he added, after another pause, "I hated her myself, Professor Musing. I thought she had left me behind. Now my father says that she didn't leave either of us. Some comfort, eh? She didn't actually walk out, because she was killed before she could."

At this Charlie rose from his seat and, a bit ridiculously, but like the gentleman he was raised to be, extended his hand. Lacking an alternative, Antigone took it. Charlie thanked her politely, said he would see her in class on Wednesday, and walked quickly out of the room.

Antigone took a deep breath at his departure. Her heart had not been in this task.

The location of her heart was precisely what Antigone's brother was pondering at this very moment. While she was finishing her lecture, and vaguely anticipating the conversation described above, Hiawatha was making his way on foot from his sister's house toward the physical plant of Clare College, where he hoped to locate Mr. Vigevano, who was, according to the chief of police, the last person to have seen Virginia Vanderlyn alive. But as he neared his destination, which he had double-checked on the little campus map that Tig had given him, Hi almost forgot where he was going. He was preoccupied, trying to reconstruct the conversation he had had with his sister the night before.

"So," Hi had begun the moment they arrived home from the bookstore. "You're absolutely convinced now that Cornelius Vanderlyn is innocent?"

Antigone sensed the veiled accusation in her brother's tone. Rather than a direct reply, she decided to counter with her own artillery.

"Hiawatha, I hope you're planning on coming home with me for Thanksgiving. When I talked to Mom the other day, it was so obvious she was longing to see you. I practically promised her I'd persuade you to come."

Hi was a bit taken aback by this dramatic change in the topic of conversation. But he gave in, and smiled. He was familiar with his sister's manipulative machinations. They were, after all, his own.

"Yes, I'll come home . . ." And this easy concession took *her* aback, "but only if you tell me right this minute what your feelings are for this Vanderlyn guy. I mean, it was pretty obvious to me, and probably to the Colonial so-called Ladies, too, that you were blushing the whole time he was talking to us. Do you think you know him well enough to have a crush on him? After all, he may or may not have killed his wife. And he hasn't done the greatest job raising that kid. And we won't even mention that he's got to be at least twenty years older than you are."

Antigone listened calmly to her brother's litany of reasons why she should not feel something for Cornelius Vanderlyn. None of them, as Hi himself must have seen, had much effect on her. But then, she was not being obstinate or evasive. She wasn't sure yet herself what she felt for Cornelius.

"The fact is, Hi, I'm not sure what I think. But I know that I like him too much for him to be a murderer. You seemed to agree yesterday."

"Yes, I think he might be innocent, but no, I don't have a crush on him, and you do," said Hi frankly, albeit with a minimum of judicial enthusiasm.

Thus the topic of sex was brought up—like the bones of Mrs. Vanderlyn, who could almost be said to have personified it—in the little living room of Antigone's cottage. And it was never the easiest topic for the brother and sister to discuss. For, if the truth be told, the middle Musing children were a rather lonely pair, sexually speaking. Neither of them were virgins, but both experienced long periods of celibacy. The reasons for this again help to characterize the differences between them.

One of the few old-fashioned ideas that Antigone subscribed to was that love and sex were inextricably entangled. For her, the sexual act was a sacred pleasure; she was attracted to the pleasure, but the sanctity put her off, or at least left her painfully shy. For Hiawatha, on the other hand, sex was a rite of passage, one that began the first time he made love—with the plump, shrewish president of his high school class—but then never really ended. It wasn't that sex led you to greater knowledge or consciousness of life; rather, it brought you face to face with an abyss, a well of never-depleted anxiety. If Antigone was slightly healthier in dealing with her longings, Hiawatha was—and only in this—slightly quieter in dealing with his. They were both aware, however, that no one has sex—or love either, for that matter—in exactly the same measure that they claim or seem to; it is either more or less. So they felt camouflaged by the general vagueness surrounding the topic, both within their family and beyond.

"I don't know," Antigone had finally responded. And with that, the conversation had been left dangling. As a result, neither Hi nor Tig had slept well last night.

Now, as Hi rounded the corner and spotted the building he was looking for, he was still worrying about how to talk to his sister. Though he could be hotheaded and overly protective, she could not doubt that he always had her best interests in mind. On more than one occasion his instincts about her male friends had turned out to be extremely accurate, though he had never—and this was the proof of his unconditional and selfless affection for her—interfered with her actions, beyond a little serious teasing, even when he thought they were wrong.

Hiawatha entered the large brick edifice, which had several enormous chimneys rising at the rear. Up and down the long central hallway, men were moving singly and in pairs, most of them clad in the blue, one-piece uniform of the manual worker. There was a reception window immediately inside; Hi tapped at the glass and asked if he could speak to a Mr. Charles Vigevano. A kind-looking, middle-aged woman turned and pressed a buzzer, which could be heard throughout the hall. After a minute or two, a young man came walking up to Hi, and told the latter that he would escort him to Chuck's office, where, a few moments later, Hi found himself alone with the head of Clare College's engineering services.

Chuck Vigevano glanced up from his desk. He was, even sitting down, a very large, imposing, robust-looking Italian in his early forties. His shirtsleeves were rolled up, exposing massive forearms and a considerable covering of black hair. His face was square, his skin a deep honey-color which betrayed his southern origins, and the hair at the top of his head was curly and black like that on his arms, only thicker and with an occasional strand of silver gray.

"What can I do for you?" Chuck asked, in a friendly but businesslike tone.

"My name is Hiawatha Musing," he began, before explaining briefly why he had come.

Because Hi had learned that it was best to include as much of the truth as possible in any lie it was necessary to tell, he followed his introduction by saying that he was staying with his sister, a colleague and friend of Professor Vanderlyn. Like everyone else, he had heard about the terrible discovery of Virginia Vanderlyn's body, and Mr. Staves, the chief of the Westerly Police, had, for reasons far too complicated to go into now, asked both Hi and his sister to follow up on anything they had heard concerning the case.

"In fact, it was Detective Staves who told us that you were the last person in Westerly to see Mrs. Vanderlyn alive." Hi ended his preamble with this rather risky misapplication of the truth. But he was so concerned with his own attempt at obtaining information concerning a murder—after all, he had no previous experience in this line of work—that he failed to notice the blood rising to the face of his interviewee.

After a leaden pause, during which Hiawatha shifted his weight nervously in his chair, Chuck Vigevano spoke.

"So, you've come for more dirt on Mrs. Vanderlyn, eh? What are you, a journalist?"

Hi was about to deny the accusation, but Vigevano gave him no time to answer.

"Well, you can just get out!" the head of engineering services roared. " 'Friend of her husband,' you say? He's going to need a friend. Because if that no-good, stuck-up asshole with all his money and his respect turns out to be the one who killed her, I'll take revenge on him myself!"

Hi didn't doubt that this southern Italian knew the meaning of revenge. He would have been happy to go without another word, but suddenly Vigevano was asking him questions.

"Do the police think it was him? Once they thought it was me! That's right. I could've killed them for suggesting it. So what do you think, Mr. Whatever-You're-Calling-Yourself? Do you think he did it?"

Hi gulped hard, and tried to remain calm. "I don't think Cornelius Vanderlyn killed her." He grew bolder, but was prepared to duck if he had to. "And I'm NOT a reporter. I only wanted to know about the last time you saw her."

Chuck squinted in disbelief. When he spoke again, it was in a mocking, sing-song voice.

"I told the police. I saw her that morning around nine. She told me that we could install her new boiler the next morning. If you're so thick with Staves, why didn't he tell you that?"

Hi ignored the last, potentially embarrassing question, asking instead, "And did you? Did you install the boiler the next day?"

"Of course not," huffed Chuck, his ire mounting again. "Mr. Vanderlyn called up and canceled. You see, if I had installed it the next morning, maybe I would have found something. Get it, Smart Boy?"

Hi had had enough. He rose, and without extending his hand, he said a quick thank you and opened the door. The other man rose, too, let out a loud expression of disgust, and slammed the door after him.

Hi, back in the street, felt a mixture of emotions, uppermost among them being relief. His heart was pounding, and his legs felt wobbly. Now there was a man with a temper, he thought, happy to be out of Mr. Vigevano's reach. And Hi had discovered one important fact, namely, that Cornelius Vanderlyn had canceled the delivery of the boiler which was due to be installed in the basement the day after Virginia disappeared. To reward himself for the successful completion of his first freelance venture into the world of criminal investigation, Hi decided to return to the comparatively warm bosom of the Colonial Ladies' bookshop, where he would retrieve and purchase, with a great show of connoisseurial authority and delight, the leather-bound edition of *The Golden Bowl*, that circumstances had previously forced him to leave behind.

XIII

DURING ANY PHASE OF LIFE, CERTAIN SETTINGS come to have a symbolic, though perhaps imprecise, significance, if only because of the frequency with which we find ourselves in them. Among the most familiar and sentiment-laden spaces we inhabit are the rooms in which we eat. Here, though we take it for granted, is sacred ground, for here lie the overlapping remains of innumerable, unforgettable but now forgotten, conversations and the spirits of the people we were on such-and-such a day, at such-and-such a period in our lives, when we felt and argued this or that point or spoke of love to so-and-so with a sincerity or a conviction now lost with the details of the menu, the faces, and the names. And there are few eating rooms which we recall at once so vaguely and so well—which, after we no longer have recourse to them, our memories overload with nostalgic meaning and an almost religious, if unacknowledged, veneration—as the college refectory or dining hall. However contemptible the food may have been, who would not give a great deal to be, for a little while anyway, the sheltered creature he or she was, among resurrected friends, partaking of that fare again?

At Clare College there were several dining rooms, but the most impressive by far was known simply as the Hall. It occupied the largest interior wing of a complex beaux-arts edifice which culminated at its vertex in a lofty, domed memorial to the military dead. Like the adjacent rotunda, the Hall was an aggressively masculine space, having been built and decorated in 1918, when the college was still attended exclusively by men. Its walls were lined with those long, horizontal photographs in black-and-white of various teams and graduating classes, images in which the individual character of each youth portrayed— and every gradation of robustness, physical beauty and mental acuity is represented—seems absorbed by, or *sacrificed to*, the larger character of the group, the proverbial sea of faces galvanized into a single expression of confidence or yearning or hope. Though women had been welcome at Clare since the nineteen-sixties, the Hall had never changed its original, men's club decor. It had retained as well the rule which made it accessible only to senior undergraduates and members of the faculty. And so it was a place that carried with it a certain prestige; it was more sedate than the other college refectories, its furnishings more refined, its food more expensive and appealing to a slightly maturer clientele.

Maturer, but only in the temporal meaning of the term. For the Hall was, above all, a favorite mealtime haunt and refuge of the faculty, due to its convenience and its freedom from underclassmen. Because they congregated here, it was also a good place to study their often unorthodox ways. We have already had reason to comment on the nervous or erratic behavior of the typical college professor, for whom every working day can be like the never-forgotten first day of kindergarten, exhilarating but also unnerving, and potentially life-determining. Even the most pompous lecturer, self-confident and with a spectacular, Ivy-clotted *curriculum vitae*, will invariably be found to possess peculiarities of conduct which render him vulnerable to contradiction, or even ridicule, in the classroom. Furthermore, it takes the resourceful undergraduate relatively little time to see that, although their teachers may indeed be brighter and

better informed, they are also necessarily handi-
capped by an inescapable self-consciousness which
more than levels the interactive field. Oddly enough,
what is true of their behavior during working hours is
magnified dramatically when they are allowed to relax
from their pedagogical duties, at mealtimes, for
instance, or with their families at weekends. As the
hypothetical subject of an anthropological study, then,
the scholastic community can be predicted with some
accuracy to provide the clearest proof that the idio-
syncrasy of thought, which is doubtless a source of
genius, is, more often than not, yoked to an idiosyn-
crasy of action, which renders the subject counter-
normal, if not positively, and by the larger world's
standards, ridiculous.

There was an excellent sampling of the ridiculous
in the Hall on this particular day. At a table directly
below the central Diocletian window—the entire
room was a slightly reduced copy of the frigidarium of
an ancient Roman bath—sat Professor Palms, from
the Department of History, a shabbily dressed sixty-
year-old who was chewing his food loudly, but who
paused every two or three minutes to make a strange,
uncomfortable face, as though on the brink of bringing up his entire meal. Three tables away to his left
was the noted Visiting Professor of Linguistics,
Maryellen Saunders, daintily devouring half a chicken

with her fingers and waving like a queen to passersby who had no idea who she was. The most colorful figure of all, perhaps, was that of the Physics Chairman, Colin McKrieg—colorful in the literal sense, for those few hues that were not represented in his mismatched attire were supplied by the fragments of food with which he seemed determined to cover everything around him—clothes, tablecloth, open books, and papers—like a cat marking its ground or a magpie selecting the best building materials for a nest.

In their midst, but hardly capable any longer of noticing their performances, sat Cornelius Vanderlyn with easy dignity, in a chair he had no doubt occupied more than once over the past thirty-five years since he had first enjoyed a meal in the Hall as a Clare senior. He was sipping his ice water. He was waiting for the colleague who had invited him to lunch. He was thinking of Virginia.

Along with the other strange effects of the discovery of his wife's body, effects such as the unprecedented desire to talk and the re-awakened need to teach, Cornelius also experienced a new aversion to sitting still. Never a man to pace or indulge in nervous habits, leg-rocking or finger-drumming, he had developed in the past five days a dread of being left idle which amounted almost to a psychosis. It was not loneliness that dogged him—he had long since domesticated that—but inactivity. Finding himself, as now, with nothing to do, even for a few moments, compelled him to conjure up his wife, who waltzed blithely back into his consciousness and gave him a queer look, expecting him to say something meaningful, and this he was at a loss to do.

Cornelius was rescued at last when a man appeared from behind, tapped him once, lightly, on his left shoulder, and hastily took a seat across from him at the little round table with its sprig of yellow freesia in the center and its heavy hotel silverware. The man was Philip Bowes. Bowes was the forty-five-year-old chairman of the Classics Department, the department in which Cornelius had spent the past two decades of his life.

Both men unfolded their napkins and placed them on their laps. Then there was an awkward silence, as they waited for one of the veteran waiters to take their order.

In appearance, Philip Bowes was far from academic. Slim, youthful, with a brilliant complexion, fine white teeth and equally fine features, he looked at once casual and aristocratic, elegant without seeming effeminate. He managed always to appear slightly, flatteringly, windblown, as though he had just stepped off a yacht. If, as we have already noted, Cornelius's handsome head most resembled a Roman

Republican bust, his lunch companion was much more like one of the Roman emperors who constituted his own field of scholastic research. In fact, Cornelius looked upon Philip Bowes now in the same way that Claudius must occasionally have looked upon his nephew, Caligula: warily, with respect but, above all, circumspection.

At last, when they had ordered their meals, the chairman spoke in a soft but manly voice.

"Thank you so much for agreeing to meet with me, Van. I can only imagine that you'd rather be left alone right now."

"On the contrary, Philip. I find I'm much happier when I have things to do. You know, it's strange, but I must confess I find myself interested in talking, for the first time in a long time—perhaps ever!" Even now Cornelius was speaking as much to himself as to his colleague.

"Well, you may find you don't want to talk to me." Bowes left the claim momentarily unsupported.

"No?" Cornelius ventured, interrogatively, after a pause of the sort which he could no longer bear.

Professor Bowes seemed to be drawing upon secret reserves of tact before finally making himself clear.

"The fact is, Van, the police have been to my house twice now. Naturally they asked a lot of questions about you. I tried to back you up at every chance they gave me. But they also asked a lot of questions about me."

Cornelius said nothing, only continued to face the chairman across their salad plates. He didn't seem anxious, nor even more than politely interested. Without assistance, Bowes went on.

"The fact is . . . The fact is, Cornelius . . ." The fact was Philip Bowes was floundering in the midst of an uncomfortable and uncharacteristic uncertainty as to how he should proceed. Finally, he seemed to erupt with his point.

"The fact is, Cornelius, that the police know that I was the man Virginia was planning to leave with when she disappeared!" He breathed again before going on. "That's right, Virginia and I were in love. I'm sorry to have to say this, especially now, but I wanted to talk to you before the police did."

The expression on Cornelius' face never changed. He took another bite of his salad, washed it down with a sip of white wine, and then dabbed his mouth with his napkin. Bowes decided that his companion must not have understood him, or else that he was, as his students might say, in denial. Even, perhaps, as the British put it, a bit round the bend. But after a moment, Cornelius disproved these hypotheses.

"And you've waited ten years to tell me this?" The question was rhetorical, and the younger man squirmed. "But, of course, I've known for ten years. That's right. And no, I'm not just saying this to save face. At first, I was a bit surprised to find you still in Westerly the day after she'd gone. Why, it must have surprised you even more than me when it turned out she had decamped. But then, when I thought more about it—as you know, I've had so much time to think—it dawned on me that you weren't really her type. I should have known. She tried to tell me. I mean, you're not the type she'd run away with."

The chairman felt as though he had been challenged and lost no time in replying.

"Oh, I think I was the type. Virginia's type, I mean."

Cornelius didn't mind playing the fool when it was a deliberate choice. But he didn't like people to think he had no alternative. His response was well-phrased and succinct.

"Dear Philip. Will you believe me when I tell you that Virginia herself told me about your affair? I suppose not. But it's the truth. She was quite apologetic, even more so than usual. And she told me, as well, that if and when she left me, it would not be for you. So you see, if you had left with her, it would have been against her will. Her own words."

Philip's face was on fire. "I was no Tarquin. And she was no Lucretia," he spat out at last.

"I don't know who or what you are, and I'm thankful it's not my job to find out. Nor do I, after all, need to spend the rest of my life trying to find out the truth about my wife. That she was *my wife* will have to suffice."

Philip Bowes pushed his plate away like the child he was at heart. Though a dynamo in the classroom, he was not famous for collegiality, especially among the larger circle of classicists who were his peers. Other people's versions of history tended to provoke his anger and jealousy. It was all he could do to remain at the table with this clever, enigmatic, and exasperating man. Finally, he took some comfort in knowing that it was not himself, but Cornelius, whom the police clearly considered the prime suspect in this case. That, after all, suited the chairman perfectly.

"Well, then," he said, after composing himself and swallowing his outrage, "I guess you knew her best. Now I only ask your forgiveness." The last line, he thought, was an excellent touch, but even so, he almost undermined himself with the hint of sarcasm he could not banish from his tone.

"Oh, I forgave you years ago," said Cornelius with insufferable tolerance. He continued to eat his meal, and Bowes considered again, with puzzled irritation, that this man must be out of his mind.

It was not, however, insanity, but a sort of humorous delight, as though he had witnessed an act of folly which had unfolded exactly according to his prediction, that twinkled in the older man's eyes. Nor did he neglect to say a polite good-bye, when, after a few more minutes had passed, the chairman rose awkwardly and walked away, leaving Cornelius alone. But not alone for long, because he was re-joined almost immediately by the ghost of Virginia, who took the seat vacated by her former lover, and cast upon her husband an unambiguous, approving smile.

XIV

HIAWATHA, STILL CLUTCHING HIS PRIZE COPY OF *The Golden Bowl,* arrived at his sister's office, his mind fairly whirring with plans for further investigation. When he knocked at the door, Antigone called to him to come in. She was just rising from her desk.

"I've been on the phone with Randall Ross. He said the police have been to talk to him and his wife, and Cornelius also called him, and he wanted to know if I needed any help with Charlie. Professor Ross, that is. I guess that the Rosses and the Vanderlyns are pretty close."

Hi was admiring his sister as she got her things together to prepare to leave. She was wearing a dark blue, knit blouse and burgundy slacks.

"You always look good in jewel tones," he complimented her. Then he immediately addressed her latest bits of information. "And do you need any help with Charlie?"

After a moment, Antigone shook her head, distractedly for her.

They left the office and headed out of the science building without a definite destination. It was just after one p.m. Tig was finished with her teaching for the day, and so they had decided to spend the afternoon doing a little sleuthing of their own—just out of curiosity, they both agreed, nothing serious. Antigone recounted her brief, uncomfortable conversation with Charlie Vanderlyn, and Hi gave a slightly exaggerated version of his set-to with the school's chief engineer.

"Tig, you would have been proud of me. The guy is at least six-foot-four, his body completely covered with hair. I mean, I think it might be. Tufts of it showed through his trouser legs. I felt like David before Goliath. I was lucky to get out alive. But now what do we do?"

"Well," said Tig, "I've agreed to have lunch with Randall Ross tomorrow, to talk about ways in which we might be of help to Professor Vanderlyn."

"Next thing you know, you'll have those two guys fighting over you. And the kid, too."

"Would that be so bad?" replied Tig in the same spirit in which Hi had made his comment.

"Well, if there's a killer loose out there, clearly you're just the man-eating Tigger to track him down." Hi spoke melodramatically, in one of his numerous television voices. "But how should we spend the afternoon?"

"Well, I thought that we might just look up one of the people Staves mentioned to us. Do you remember? He said something about Virginia having a good friend, a librarian named Hermione Pole. I don't think we could get into trouble if we went and introduced ourselves. In fact, call it instinct, but I wouldn't be surprised if Staves intended for us to look her up. He's too clever to drop a name accidentally, especially when he could see how curious you are."

"And I'm not the only one. I'm sure he could also see that you've fallen in love with the prime suspect. Hey, I've been thinking. You're sure you're not just in love with all his stuff? Maybe it's not Cornelius Vanderlyn you like, but his fancy antiquities. The dagger Brutus used to stab Caesar, and Cleopatra's false eyelashes. I mean, I wouldn't blame you if you were. But my silence is going to cost you."

"Oh, Hi, no price would be too great," his sister laughed. And they made their way across campus to the library.

The Henry Besserman Farr Memorial Library was built at the end of the nineteenth century in a flamboyant Gothic style, according to the wishes of the man who paid for it, Henry Besserman Farr. Mr. Farr was a self-made man, a millionaire who had left school in the fifth grade. Late in life, and as though in thanks for not having been impeded in his commercial pursuits by a prolonged education, he made an enormous grant to the college in Westerly. This grant resulted in one of the country's largest and most beautiful private libraries for Clare, and, for Mr. Farr, the total estrangement of his extensive family. Their loss, however, continued to be Clare's gain, because right up to his death, in 1911, Mr. Farr continued to enrich the library with the priceless volumes which are only one reason for its fame. And it was in the special division devoted to the care of rare books that Hermione Pole worked.

When Hi and Tig arrived at the library, however, she was out to lunch.

"Well, if we had planned ahead, we could have had our own picnic in the courtyard while we waited for Miss Pole," said Antigone.

"I've thought of that," said Hi proudly, reaching into the soft leather briefcase he was rarely without. Antigone knew from experience that this bag always contained a shocking number of sometimes even more shocking things. Now, he withdrew two sandwiches wrapped in paper, and after handing them to Tig, he took out two large, perfect apples.

"To the courtyard," he said, and his sister smilingly led him to the beautiful cloistered space in the heart of the library complex. It was, they were happy to find, completely deserted. They had their choice from among four or five benches, settling, after a semi-serious argument about the relative benefits and dangers of sunlight, on a compromise at the base of an ancient elm tree, half under and half out of the shade.

The silence, like the chicken salad sandwiches and the apples, was delectable. It seemed protected by the low arches of honey-colored stone that surrounded them on three sides. On the fourth side, the wall of a tower rose many stories, its surface stained in various places by the creeping patterns of ivy, now turned luminous and hardly plausible shades of acid orange and cerise. And in the center of the courtyard was a small fountain, really no more than a large bowl with a trickle of water rising out of a metal spigot in the middle. It had been salvaged from a comparably cloistered space in the original eighteenth-century library. Just below the circular lip of the lead basin was etched the year, 1769, followed by a couplet in old script:

Whom the Sounde of these Waters Reaches
Abydes in a Paradyse of Wordes.

Hi eyed the fountain, in between bites of apple.

"Tig," he finally asked, "how big do you think that fountain is?"

Antigone was immediately suspicious.

"Why?" she asked warily.

"Well, I just wondered if we came back at night, do you think we could fit it into the trunk of your car?"

"Hi!" she exclaimed. She was painfully aware of her brother's bad habit of selecting technically unavailable souvenirs of his life experiences. Though he usually restricted himself to hotel bath towels or transfer ware dinner plates, in college he had once made off with a five-light candelabrum from the campus chapel, where he had attended the wedding of a former roommate. She thought that he had given up the practice, but just in case, she admonished him now.

"Don't even think about it! First of all, it would probably qualify as grand theft. Secondly, do you really want Detective Staves investigating YOU?"

"I was only joking," Hi announced, never taking his eyes from the fountain; his tone suggested he was still speculating as to the measurements of the piece.

When at last they had finished their lunch, and taken, at Hi's insistence, a closer look at some of the carved capitals of the stocky pillars between the arches—these were chiseled to represent a variety of real and imaginary creatures, and Tig was relieved to find that none of them were loose—they returned to the rare book department, where they were introduced by a subordinate to Miss Hermione Pole. When they explained that they had come to ask her about Virginia Vanderlyn, she conducted them to a room away from the prying eyes of incunabulaphiles; it was, in fact, her office, a large, wood-paneled space filled with neat piles of old manuscripts and the leather or vellum bindings from which they had become separated.

"I sort them out and select the ones that need restoration," said the librarian, following the eyes of her younger companions, who were impressed by the sheer quantity of the ancient volumes. Then she made a large gesture, and the three of them sat down around Hermione's enormous library desk.

Hermione Pole was by no means the stereotypical lady librarian. She did not wear cats-eye bifocals on a chain, nor a set of pearls over a high, lace-collared blouse or chastely buttoned, hand-knit sweater. She was a slight, upright woman whose clothes, in fact, were incongruously chic for her occupation; today she was wearing a pleated black Dior skirt and a white silk blouse that must have been tailored to her body. She was, furthermore, very thoughtful and deliberate in her movements—though occasionally she tossed her head and fluttered her hands—but she gave no indication of being too narrowly focused in her mind, the way so many librarians are. Clearly in late middle age, with her hair dyed blond and a knowing look on her delicate, lightly-powdered face, Hi and Tig were delighted to find her so friendly and insightful. And they were most delighted to find she was a talker.

"Yes, Virginia and I were very good friends. I think I can say that I was her best friend here at the college." She smiled, and her smile, like the rest of her, was small, neat, polite, and pleasing, and put Hi in mind of an eighteenth-century Meissen shepherdess. "But tell me, what is your interest in the matter?"

Hi and Tig looked at each other, and Hi wisely allowed his sister to respond.

"Well, to be frank, ours is more personal curiosity," Antigone began honestly. "I teach chemistry here at the college, and one of my students is Charlie Vanderlyn. My brother and I have become acquainted with his father. And Detective Staves has asked us for some assistance."

Antigone left exactly the right number of holes in her explanation of how she and her brother had become involved in the case, and Hermione seemed not to worry about filling them.

"Yes, poor Charlie," the older woman sighed. "Of course, I've already talked to your detective about my friendship with Virginia. But they never let me get a word in about Charlie. You see, all the police were interested in was any information I could give them concerning the men Virginia had slept with."

Hi and Tig considered blushing here, but as Hermione gave no hint that she felt it was necessary, they forbore. She went on.

"So I provided them with a list, and then they seemed disappointed it wasn't longer. They went off before I could make my confession, so to speak."

Hi and Tig leaned closer to her.

"About Charlie. You see, it was I who sent all those cards. I couldn't believe that Virginia had left without her child. So that first year, as his birthday drew near, and then passed, I decided I would send him a card and sign her name. I had her handwriting to look at so I just wrote "Love Mum." I worried about it, but at the same time I felt that Virginia would probably thank me if she knew. It really astonished me and disappointed me that she never wrote to him. But then, how could anyone doubt that she had actually left? I mean, there was that note that everyone had heard about, and no one seemed to question. So each year—it became a habit—I sent him one or two cards, each with a little present. Although I had never been particularly friendly with his father—I'm afraid I haven't any patience for fools—I did see him at school, and I made a point of asking after the boy. I even went out of my way to pass by his own school now and then, and more than once I saw him playing in the yard. I continued to send him these birthday and Christmas cards—I don't have any family of my own, you know—and, as I've said, I vaguely thought that when I did see Virginia again, for I never doubted I would, she would thank me for having done that for her."

Hiawatha and Antigone were both rapt with attention, enjoying what was becoming an addictive rush of satisfaction at the hearing of hitherto undivulged information. So this refined and elegant woman, seated among her battered breviaries and broken spines, had adopted, with a few untroubled strokes of the pen, the dead woman's child. Tig was filled with admiration for her, while Hi was filled with disdain for Mr. Staves, who hadn't bothered to let the woman tell her tale. But, of course, there were more questions to be answered.

"And when she left," Hi began cautiously, afraid of affecting in any way the librarian's volubility, "you were completely surprised? That is, she hadn't confided her plans to you?"

Antigone looked approvingly at her brother, and they both turned to Hermione for her reply.

"Well, I suppose I always knew she was going to leave. Only not, of course, in the way it turns out she did." She paused here, not for a show of sadness, but as an unaffected indication of the connection she would always feel with her departed friend. "I can tell you that whatever their relationship, she wasn't about to leave for Philip Bowes."

"Philip Bowes?" said Antigone.

"He's the present chairman of Van's department. Cornelius's department, that is. Classics. He was a fast-talking young scholar who had only arrived the year before Virginia's departure. They had a very brief encounter. He couldn't get over it. He was becoming a pest."

"Had they become enemies?" Hi ventured.

"I think he was too dense and too egotistical to see how Virginia felt," Hermione explained. "But if you're looking for enemies, there were a few, as I told Police Chief Staves. For example, there was that ridiculous woman, Judy Wagner Dumont. She came to Clare at the same time as Virginia. She started out as a secretary in Cornelius's department, and from the very first, it was clear that she was looking for a faculty husband. She was wildly in love with Cornelius and made no secret of it and of her commiseration with him for having such a wife. To his credit, Cornelius never gave her the time of day, but that only inflamed her more. Virginia told me that the crazy woman had actually tried to blackmail her! She said she had proof that Virginia had 'slept around.' That's

what Miss Wagner called it. It's anybody's guess
where she was brought up. Anyway, Virginia just
laughed at her."

Antigone recognized the name of Judy Dumont;
Charlie had mentioned her as an unwelcome sympa-
thizer of his father's.

"And what is her relationship now, do you think,
with Charlie and his father?" Antigone asked with
studied indifference.

"From what I hear, she can't leave them alone.
Even though she did eventually marry a lecturer in
the Freshman Humanities Program, a Mr. Dumont—
who has yet to receive his doctoral degree—she still
pesters the Vanderlyns constantly, turning up at Cornelius's apartment with cookies and frozen casseroles,
things I'm sure he wouldn't touch."

"Might she have hated Virginia enough to . . ."
began Hi, solemnly.

"To kill her? Impossible." Hermione was
adamant. "The woman hasn't the capacity, mental or
otherwise. And besides, a lot of women disliked Virginia, a lot of women smarter than Judy Wagner
Dumont. Mrs. Hughes, to begin with, had every reason
to hate her, as her husband, Professor Hughes—he was
the chairman of Classics at the time Cornelius joined
the department and after his marriage to Virginia—had
been chasing her around for years. Pathetically, I might

add." Apparently, Hermione had a singular contempt for all of the men in Virginia's life. But then, she evinced an equally polite contempt for most women, too.

"Who do you think may have murdered her?" Hi could no longer contain his curiosity.

At this question, Hermione seemed to retreat into herself for the first time in the interview. Was this reticence the reluctance of a conscientious woman to point the finger without proof, or was she hiding something? Neither Antigone nor Hiawatha could tell for sure. But her answer was distinctly ambiguous.

"Oh, I can think of many people who would have liked to hurt Virginia, but not the one who could."

With that, the discussion came to a close. Brother and sister thanked the librarian profusely for her time and proceeded out of the library toward Antigone's cottage. On the way there, they had a lively conversation, considering the information they had just obtained.

"Hermione was certainly a mine, wasn't she?" said Hi excitedly.

"I'll say," his sister agreed. "But I think there's even more where that came from. Did you notice how she clammed up at the end? I'll bet she has a good idea who the guilty party is."

"And what if it's Cornelius?" Hi asked again. He briefly considered telling his sister what Chuck had told him about the new boiler being canceled. That might be the proof that Cornelius didn't want anyone in the basement. But, in the end, he merely added, "Hermione certainly doesn't like him."

"I don't think Miss Pole likes men at all, though I can't say she was a spokesperson for women, either. I wonder what, exactly, drew her and Virginia together? Maybe I'll ask Randall Ross tomorrow at lunch. By the way, what will you be doing at that time? Do you want to come with me?"

But Hi had other ideas, which he was eager to share with his sister.

"Well, I've just been thinking, and it sounds like a visit to this Judy Wagner Dumont might be interesting. It's better if I see her alone, since she's a rival of yours for Cornelius, and I wouldn't want to be in the middle of a cat fight." Hiawatha elbowed his sister gently.

"But eventually, Hi, we're going to get into trouble. I mean, Mrs. Dumont may wonder what right you have to be questioning her about this or any other matter."

"Yes, that's been worrying me, too, but I've finally thought of something. When he saw me, Chuck Vigevano practically insisted that I was a journalist, so maybe that's what I should be. My guess is that this Dumont person is dying to have her say about Virginia Vanderlyn, so I'll tell her I'm writing a human interest story for some newspaper or other about the effects of the recent police discovery, etcetera, etcetera. I mean, she doesn't know me from Adam. And from what old Hermione had to say, she'll be only too happy to slander the poor ex-Vanderlyn and maybe give us a scoop on the worthy Cornelius, as well."

"But Hi, you don't look or act anything like a journalist." Antigone was laughing.

"So say you," said Hiawatha, unruffled. "But I'll change my manners and my appearance. For example, I'll wear an old pair of spectacles that I always carry with me, just in case."

Antigone's approval of the obsolete term "spectacles" could not be extended to her brother's plan for concealment. She had a vague recollection of the glasses he had in mind, a hideous pair with thick, black, horn rims which he had originally worn during his senior year in high school, while he was in his French-film-director phase. She did not think that an intended resemblance to Francois Truffaut could possibly convince Ms. Dumont, dumb as she was reputed to be, to disburden herself to Hi. When, at last, they reached the door of Tig's house, she was preparing herself to spend the entire evening, if necessary, trying to talk her brother out of his impossible scheme.

XV

THE NEXT MORNING, LONG AFTER HIS SISTER HAD left to teach her last class before the Thanksgiving holidays, Hiawatha emerged from the house feeling refreshed and ready for another day of amateur investigation. He was, indeed, wearing his infamous horn-rimmed glasses. He had been dismayed, but not deterred, when he discovered, after looking through his suitcase for them, that one of the lenses was missing. But, he reasoned, he could just pop out the other one, and if he kept his distance, no one would be the wiser. Only one minor problem remained: however these lens-less glasses may have helped him, in his own mind, to play a role, they did nothing to reduce his myopia, so that when, for example, he mounted the stairs to the entrance of Judy Wagner Dumont's apartment building, he took exaggerated steps, afraid of tripping on the blurry treads.

When he knocked at the door of Mrs. Dumont's apartment, he was greeted by a yell from within, which reached him over the blare of a television set.

"Who is it?"

"It's Mr. Musing, the journalist," responded Hi, in a voice somewhat deeper than usual. "I called this morning, and you told me you could see me at eleven-thirty."

The television snapped off, and a moment later the door was opened.

"Hello," said Hi. "I'm Hiawatha Musing." And he extended his hand.

Judy Wagner Dumont was one of that category of women who, when they are young, are referred to ambiguously as pixies. When they reach middle age, it is hard to know what to call them. Mrs. Dumont was now in her late forties and bore all the vestigial signs of the former pixie: she was short, with short black hair, and chubby limbs, and large teeth in a round face. She moved about a great deal, spoke very quickly in a rather grating tone, and seemed to be just barely managing to contain a potentially threatening energy, like a lit firecracker in a Mason jar.

"Come in, come in," she said, waving him into the apartment. "I don't want the neighbors to see I'm giving an interview." And she glanced quickly down the length of the deserted corridor.

Mrs. Dumont led Hiawatha into the kitchen, offered him some coffee, which he declined politely, and then sat across from him at the Formica-topped table. The apartment was a medium-sized, modern dwelling, the walls decorated with a profusion of pre-framed, reproduction *fin-de-siècle* Parisian posters. Directly behind Ms. Dumont's head, Jane Avril spread her skirts promiscuously.

"Hiawatha?" queried Judy. "I always thought that was a girl's name!" And she emitted a sharp, resonant giggle.

"Well, in fact, Hiawatha was a great Mohawk chief. Not to mention the famous MALE subject of the Longfellow poem." Hi was slightly put out.

"If you say so," bellowed Judy patronizingly. "Now let's get down to business. First of all, what paper do you write for?"

Hiawatha had anticipated the question.

"The Boston Sun Times," he replied, with a convincing mixture of nonchalance and occupational pride.

"Well, I've never heard of that," Judy eyed him sharply.

"We're rather new. It's with stories like this that we hope to make our name. You know, stories of real people, honestly told, without all the usual media distortion and advertising."

Mrs. Dumont thought for a moment, then lunged a little across the table. The move brought her uncomfortably close to her guest.

"Hey, this isn't a tabloid, is it?"

"Believe me, I do not write for a tabloid," responded Hi, with all of the honest man's conviction.

Mrs. Dumont continued to peer into his eyes.

"Say, there aren't any lenses in your glasses!"

"Of course there are," Hiawatha assured her, putting a greater distance between the two of them. "They're the latest in non-glare, micro-thin plastic. Very expensive. Now, Mrs. Dumont, IS there anything you would like to share with the world concerning the Vanderlyn case?"

"Boy, is there!" She settled back in her chair. "I've already told my story to the police, of course, because, after all, I've known Cornelius Vanderlyn for years. Even before he was married. We used to work together, you know." She looked rather emotional as she said this.

"In what capacity, exactly, did you know Cornelius Vanderlyn?" continued Hi.

"Well, I was an administrative assistant in the Classics Department. We were very close, Van and I. I mean, we still are, except that I don't see him as often anymore, since I got married and became a faculty wife."

"When was that?" asked Hi, who couldn't have cared less, but knew that he must strive to seem interested in his source for her own sake.

"Oh, about five years ago. But I still visit him now and then. He's so lonely, poor man, and the woman who cleans for him is useless. Sometimes I bring him food, just so he can have a decent meal. And of course I know Charlie, too. I feel almost like a mother to that boy." Again she appeared on the brink of expressing emotions which would have been at odds with her harsh, staccato manner of speaking.

"And his wife, Mrs. Vanderlyn . . . Did you know her as well?" Hi asked at last.

"Well, not the way some people did, that's for sure!" And when she said this, Judy Wagner Dumont produced a highly original version of a leer.

"Yes?" Hiawatha wanted her to continue.

"Oh, I'm not one to speak ill of the dead, but Virginia Vanderlyn definitely got what she deserved. The way she treated Cornelius. All those men!" She pronounced these last words loudly and with prolonged emphasis. "Not to mention that she was a total bitch to me!"

"Well, I have heard that there were affairs. But is that so unusual in academia?" asked Hi, feigning uncertainty.

"Yes, but with students? And the number of men she ran around with was mind-boggling." Judy seemed to be under a spell, envisioning the endless parade of Virginia's lovers. Then she came back to herself. "Say, shouldn't you be writing this down?"

Hi had, in fact, neglected to take out his notebook to record what he learned, though he hastily corrected the situation now, asking simultaneously after the specifics of Mrs. Vanderlyn's affairs.

"Well," Judy began again, "there was old Professor Hughes, who just retired last year, and Mark Simmons—he's the one Cornelius found in the shower. There was Jack Shapiro in Biology—he died a few years ago. There were at least a couple of others I didn't know. The student's name was Paul something. Mullaney, I think. And it's so weird, too, because she wasn't even particularly attractive. She had a crooked front tooth. Not one at the very front, but you could definitely see it."

"It's funny, I've been told she was quite a beauty," Hi suggested, unwittingly contradicting her.

Judy moved closer to him again, ostensibly ignoring his comment. "Are you sure there are really lenses in those glasses?" She was, by nature, suspicious, and now she was growing more so.

"I've told you, yes," said Hi, his head down now, writing in a furious illegible shorthand.

"I think maybe you should show me some identi-fication before we go on. I know when my sister in Albany was . . . er . . . tangentially involved in a crime, and the press interviewed her, they all had special identification. And by the way, how much will I get paid for this story?"

Hiawatha's entire body broke out in a cold sweat. "Well, we don't pay for our interviews. As I said, we're a very young newspaper."

This was as much as Mrs. Dumont needed to hear.

"Right!" she shouted, "you can have the interview when you show me some I.D. And I'm not talking for free."

"Well, Mrs. Dumont, I could speak to my editors, and they might be able to arrange . . ." Hi had no idea where he was headed with this line. But it didn't mat-ter, as the woman didn't give him time to finish it.

"Okay, call them right now. There's the phone. I'll wait," she said, with a rabid look on her fat little face and her bobbed hair rising as though from a static electrical charge.

"Well, it would probably be better if I spoke to them in person."

"Right!" she said again, leaping up from her chair. "Out!"

Hi gulped, but immediately rose from his seat. He quickly gathered up the notebook and reached on the floor for his briefcase, which he might have retrieved faster if he had been able to see better where it was. Then, before he knew what was happening, the woman was hustling him out of the kitchen. Twice he felt her finger poke him in the back.

"Boston Sun Times, my ass!" he heard her shout.

And then the door slammed behind him.

XVI

A T EXACTLY THE SAME MOMENT THAT HIAWATHA WAS being ignominiously expelled by Judy Wagner Dumont, Antigone was finishing her lunch with Randall Ross. They had eaten in a small, modern cafeteria on the ground floor of the large administrative building at the center of the campus.

Their conversation had been a quiet but informative one. So far, Antigone had obtained a number of insights into the characters of both Cornelius and Virginia, although Ross provided them in a characteristically teasing way. They were, at least to begin with, a loving couple—and all loving couples are ill-fated. They fought—but all couples fought. They both adored Charlie—but Charlie would have been better off living away from them. Ross told several anecdotes to illustrate his version of the Vanderlyn home-life, with which he had been intimately acquainted. He was interested, clearly, in the fate of his friend Cornelius, but he seemed unwilling to take seriously the notion that anyone might suspect the latter of a crime. And with regard to Virginia's reputation, he was philosophical and suggestive.

"Well, I suppose we all leave a trail of victims in our wake," sighed the handsome professor, with mock solemnity.

"Now you sound like Cornelius Vanderlyn," Antigone noted aloud.

"Is that so surprising? We're from the same generation, and though we're not ancient, it's a different generation from yours. Take their marriage, for example. Cornelius and Virginia got married when? Around 1980? For people who were raised in the sixties and seventies, there was a kind of glamour attached to adultery. Marital open-mindedness came to be considered a virtue, at least in theory." Here Professor Ross grinned sheepishly, adding, "Not, of course, that anybody really wanted to be cheated on. But to cheat, that was a mark of sophistication."

Antigone looked as though she wasn't convinced.

"Yes, really," Ross went on. "Just think about it. Nowadays we hear about homosexuals wanting to marry. Well, if you ask me, what they really want is the opportunity to commit adultery. No, I don't mean that in any homophobic or politically incorrect way. But think about it. If, from a legal standpoint, they are prevented from being unfaithful at that level, at the level of actual criminality which is officially looked down upon by the same society which, to judge from television or the tabloids, finds nothing on earth more fascinating and attractive—why, that's a whole world of profound and disturbing emotions that are left inaccessible to them. It's like not being allowed to take a test—a test which, especially if you fail, carries with it strange raptures of sensuality and guilt."

Yes, Antigone thought, Professors Ross and Vanderlyn had a great deal in common. They were both, above all, people who knew how to talk, and, she privately acknowledged, such individuals were far less common in the Sciences. Antigone was only partly seduced by Ross's oratorical skills, however. She was less interested in the issue of homosexual marriage, with which, incidentally, she had no problem, than she was in a question that had only recently entered her mind.

"And do you think Cornelius believes that, too? Do you think he acted on it?" she asked a little furtively.

"Oh, I think there were women. Would that have been so bad, given his circumstances?"

Antigone couldn't commit herself.

"But I thought he was so in love with Virginia. You said yourself they were a loving couple much of the time."

"Well, at the beginning, yes, but that never lasts. And Cornelius's devotion to Virginia has been exaggerated. He knew who she was. That fact alone should help to exculpate him. Cornelius is not a passionate man. And certainly not the kind of man who could kill for love."

Antigone was thinking. She had a slightly different view of Cornelius, but, admittedly, less familiarity with him. Now she was concentrating her efforts on not registering visibly the disappointment she felt at Ross's implication that Cornelius had had his own adulterous affairs.

As though reading her mind, her companion spoke up.

"But listen, we've talked enough about the Vanderlyns. Let's talk about you and your brother. I thought his paper was splendid. You were right to let

me know that he would be applying for the conference. Though, of course, I didn't tell him that."

"Yes, and thank you again from both of us. He
only needs a little more confidence in himself,"
replied Tig, getting up from the table as the sound of
the nearby carillon struck one. She was still pondering
the news about Cornelius.

Randall Ross rose, too. He took Tig's elbow and
walked with her out of the lunchroom.

"By the way, are you and your brother fixed up for
Thanksgiving? Because Laura and I would be
delighted if you came to our house."

At the mention of his wife, Antigone automatically, though she didn't know why, thought of Virginia again. Not that she had ever really stopped
thinking about her.

"I suppose the whole thing has really upset your
wife?" she asked, a bit distractedly.

"Laura is an intelligent woman, and being an
intelligent woman, the interest she takes in the world
is minimal." Ross said this frankly, and without the
least sarcasm or criticism. "But what do you say,
about Thanksgiving?"

"Oh, I'm sorry. Thank you, but I've finally convinced Hi to come home with me to Boston. Actually,
it turned out to be surprisingly easy."

"Uh-oh," Ross reacted. "'Convinced him' doesn't sound too good. Family problems?"

"Oh it's nothing, really," said Tig, not wanting to bother her friend with personal matters, despite the fact that she felt very comfortable talking to him. And in any case, how could she begin to explain the puzzling self-destructiveness of her family, which always threatened her peace of mind? Hi and Tig had long tried to maintain secrecy with regard to that aspect of their lives. It was no doubt this secrecy which suggested to outsiders the collapse of their domestic background. And it was precisely in a state of collapse that Hi and Tig viewed it, for although not even their nicknames were taken from Poe, both lived with the vague feeling that their family life most resembled the House of Usher.

"Well, if you can't make it on Thursday, we're having a little party to kick off the holidays on Saturday evening. Around eight o'clock. Don't worry about letting us know. Just come if you can. Bring Hiawatha, but please leave Detective Staves behind."

They both chuckled. Then Antigone said goodbye, and was taken slightly aback when Ross kissed her on the cheek, rather close to the mouth. Taken aback, but not displeased. He had kissed her once before like that, several months ago. While Antigone quelled her confused reactions, Professor Ross headed away in the direction of his office.

Antigone was even more thoughtful than usual as she strolled back to her house. She felt that the more she learned about the Vanderlyns, the less objective she was able to be. It was not that she was as attached to the idea of Cornelius's innocence as her brother seemed to think—though she still believed in it—but there was a fog around the principal characters involved in the murder. The jovial Professor Ross, with whom she felt genuinely at ease, had told her a great deal today about his unfortunate friends, but it had not cleared things up. On the contrary, it had rather served to confuse them. Antigone considered briefly whether Ross himself might not have gone to bed with Virginia. But he spoke of her so calmly that she thought this was unlikely. And his wife, the detached and aloof Laura—had she possibly slept with Cornelius? Ross's image of the hedonistic nine-teen-eighties suddenly left her suspecting everyone. She estimated momentarily how much she had missed by never participating in an orgy—for there had been a few in college, but she had never been tempted.

It was in a relatively unfamiliar state of nervous anxiety, mindlessly fingering the top button of her blouse, that Antigone arrived home, unlocked her door, and walked in.

XVII

ALMOST IMMEDIATELY UPON ARRIVING HOME FROM her lunch with Professor Ross, when she had not yet had time to kick off her shoes or pour herself a glass of water, Tig heard her doorbell ring. She assumed that it would be her brother, because, though she had given him a spare key, she knew from experience that he would probably have forgotten he had it. When she opened the door, however, she saw that it was not Hiawatha, but Detective Staves. He was smiling, as usual.

"Hello, Professor Musing One. I've come to talk to you and Professor Musing Two. May I come in?"

Antigone made way for the police chief, explaining that she had only arrived home moments ago, and that she wasn't sure where her brother was. Meanwhile, Hiawatha himself, who had, in fact, remembered his key, came out from his bedroom.

"I just got in," he explained. "I was changing my clothes, and I heard my sister at the door." He seemed almost to be testifying to his recent activities, and only briefly looked directly at Detective Staves. As they moved together toward the living room, the latter stopped and addressed them both.

"Well, to begin with, a Mrs. Judith Dumont has called my office to complain that a strange man with false glasses has been harassing her." Staves was not smiling when he spoke these words.

Hiawatha turned pale. He had only just come from the Dumont residence. How could the woman have moved so quickly? thought Hi. But then he remembered that she was an ex-pixie. Still, Hiawatha's visit could hardly be construed as harassment.

"You know, if you were younger, I would spank you," continued Staves, frowning now, and looking directly at Hi. And he meant it, too, for, as the father of five children between the ages of twelve and nineteen, Staves was fast growing nostalgic for the days when control could be so easily maintained.

Hiawatha's cheeks flamed. He hated to be treated like a child, or even to be reminded, by anyone outside his family, that he had ever been one. Still, he had become too involved in this case to risk being forced to renounce it altogether by arguing with the chief of police. So he said nothing.

It was Antigone who broke the silence with a laugh. "Yes, well, I doubt if there's time for that. You see, Detective Staves, I'm convinced—I mean, my brother and I are convinced—that there is a lot more to this case than even the police can imagine. We were thinking that since we're academics and consequently already on the inside, so to speak, we might continue to help in some way. For example, . . ."

But the police chief cut her off.

"I hate to sound predictable, and talk like a television detective—you know how I hate that—but I'm afraid you've been taking liberties. Both of you. I don't mind your trying to help, and I realize that I myself am partly to blame. But when I asked you to talk to Charlie," here he looked directly at Tig, "I only thought that you would want to make this whole thing easier on the kid."

"And that's the only reason I agreed to do it," said Tig, and there was a sharp righteousness in her voice which surprised both her brother and herself. She tried to maintain it as she went on. "But now that I've done what you asked, I feel it only fair to act upon what I've learned."

"And exactly what have you learned?" asked the detective, staving off momentarily his inclination to conclude his reprimand and put an end to the interference of the "curious pair."

"I've written down, as well as I could remember it, the conversation I had with Charlie Vanderlyn." Tig walked briskly past the detective toward her briefcase in the hall and extracted from it a manila folder. "As you'll see when you've read it, the boy really cares about his father and clearly thinks he's being victimized by suspicious, unintelligent minds."

Hi made a loud snort, which he immediately regretted, as his sister was handling the situation so well. Tig didn't look at him, but continued.

"The same minds who, coincidentally, victimized his mother, both before and after her death. There are a number of people you should be looking into. As far as I'm concerned . . ." And only at this point did Antigone falter.

Staves pushed her to offer a conclusion he was sure he already knew, but it was Hiawatha who took over here.

"And we're both convinced that Cornelius Vanderlyn is completely innocent," he blurted out before exchanging with his sister a meaningful glance, one which expressed relief on both their parts.

"Perhaps we could sit down," suggested the detective, who, after listening to the siblings, had slowly reassumed his characteristic, if now slightly fatigued, smile.

The three of them moved into the living room and seated themselves, with Staves in the middle of the sofa flanked by the two academics. Immediately, the brother and sister bombarded the chief of police with details of their respective interviews with Charlie Vanderlyn, Chuck Vigevano, Judy Dumont, and Randall Ross. They took turns, all along aware of the risk they were running by admitting to most of these meetings. Finally, and almost in unison, as though they had practiced it in advance, they unveiled their *pièce-de-résistance*, the conversation they had had with Hermione Pole, and the fact, hitherto undivulged to the police, that she had been the person who had written to Charlie in Virginia's name, after the latter's disappearance. Then they added their conviction that Miss Pole knew more than she had said. Staves stroked the burgeoning stubble on his chin. There was no way around it; in some respects he was like a fictional detective. At last, he spoke.

"Are you finished? Yes? Good. Now, in the first place, let me congratulate you both on your enthusiasm, and on the ingenuity with which you wheedled your way into the lives of perfect strangers and somehow managed to make them talk. Of course, I know you would never misrepresent yourselves, so I can only assume that you charmed their secrets out of them. But, although I have no desire to hurt your feelings, I must explain to you that almost every-thing you've told me, I already knew. And you've also left out a few important things. For example, Hiawatha, you neglected to remind me that Cornelius Vanderlyn had canceled the order for the new boiler within hours of his wife's disappearance."

Hiawatha winced internally when Staves made this announcement, as he had not yet mentioned the detail to his sister. It was, after all, not necessarily significant.

Staves noted Hi's expression, then proceeded with his speech.

"Granted that we haven't yet had time to talk at length to the lady librarian . . ."

The detective's old-fashioned, and slightly sarcastic, reference to Hermione Pole suggested to Hi and Tig that, with regard to this one piece of information at least, they had upstaged the police.

"Nevertheless, we have gathered almost enough evidence to make an arrest. And without going into the specifics, I must tell you that you are wasting your time. Furthermore, I must warn you that any future interference would be a serious matter, not to mention potentially dangerous to yourselves. And it's my job to make sure no one else gets hurt. I wouldn't hesitate to toss you both into the clink if I thought it was for your own good."

The police chief's tone when he made this speech was a perfect mixture of paternal solicitude and firmness. The expression on his face was similarly split, the lower half still smiling, but in the upper half, his brows were knit, his eyes fixed and stern. Hi, who had a history of being easily bullied, was almost ready to give in, preoccupied as he was gradually becoming with the swift approach of the holidays and his hasty promise to accompany his sister home. Tig's reaction was less easy to read. Finally, exchanging one more look with her brother, she responded to all that Staves had said.

"Thank you, Mr. Staves, for your concern. Of course, if it's a matter of our protection, I'm sure you're right to tell us to stop interfering. And as we'll be leaving Westerly tomorrow for the holidays, well, it certainly makes sense for us to leave everything up to you."

Thus, Antigone made what appeared to be a perfect gesture of concession, the bowing out of an amateur before the greater wisdom and experience of the professional. But Hi recognized immediately what the detective possibly did not, namely, that this was only a performance on his sister's part. Clearly, she had something up her sleeve, and Hi found his own interest in the case, which had so obviously flagged under the glare of male authority a moment ago, reviving and even increasing with his admiration for his sister.

Staves, after a pause which was not completely devoid of wariness, finally put his hands on his knees and rose from the couch.

"Well, then, I'll thank you again for talking to Charlie, and we'll say no more about the other incidents. And just in case I don't see you before the holidays—I won't, will I?—I'll wish you a happy Thanksgiving. Oh, and by all means, Mr. Musing, do stop by if you're ever in town again. Without your disguise, of course. I would hate not to recognize you."

With this final tweak, and apparently satisfied with the results of their conversation, the policeman left the house and drove off. Antigone immediately closed the door and turned to Hi.

"Quick!" she said, running toward her bedroom. "Put some shoes on!" Hi had only socks on his feet. "And grab your jacket, because it's getting chilly."

"Why?" asked her brother excitedly. "Where are we going?" But he followed his sister toward the sleeping quarters of the house.

"We're going to pay a call on the former chairman of Cornelius's department, Professor Armitage Quincy Hughes."

XVIII

A ND SO ANTIGONE AND HIAWATHA FOUND THEM-SELVES knocking at the door of yet another faculty home, that of the Hughes family. On their way there, Hi had found it difficult to keep up with his sister. They were on foot again, as they had been when they visited the Vanderlyn house, but this time Antigone was in the lead. Her brother asked her a number of questions on the way; but more than information, he wanted some sort of reassurance that what they were doing was a good idea.

"But Staves is going to kill us if he finds out we're still rooting around," Hi suggested faintheartedly. He found the detective more than a little daunting.

"Nonsense," said Antigone, maintaining her pace. "We have a perfect right to call on our colleagues. If they won't talk to us, that's another thing. We'll deal with that if we have to. And even a refusal to talk is a kind of admission of something."

"But why the Hugheses?" Hi was only trying to slow his intrepid sister down.

"Because they keep turning up in conversations about Virginia. You just told me that the Dumont woman named Professor Hughes as one of Virginia's lovers. And Hermione Pole said the same thing, and seemed to suspect Mrs. Hughes as well. Hi, try to keep up. We've only got twenty-four hours before we leave for home!"

The mention of home, more than the logic of her arguments, caused Hi to keep quiet, though it didn't quicken his step. He was silent for the rest of the journey, torn between an intense, instinctive curiosity and an equally strong inclination to return to the safety of his sister's sofa in front of the TV. But he did make one more inquiry.

"But how do you know they'll be home?"

"Hiawatha, you know as well as I do that once a professor retires, and they give him his emeritus badge, they take away his office, and he's never allowed on campus again. Where else does he have to go?" This seemed to Hi a bit exaggerated, if not downright specious, but Tig followed it up with something more concrete. "Besides, I looked up the address, and walked past the house on my way back from school. There was a car in the driveway. Somebody's home."

Sure enough, there was a ten-year-old Toyota in the drive outside the Hughes house, and when they knocked on the front door, a uniformed maid opened it.

"Hello, my name is Professor Musing. Antigone Musing. This is my brother, also Professor Musing. We were wondering if we might talk to Professor or Mrs. Hughes. It's a fairly important matter. Is either of them at home?"

The Hispanic woman, small and crisply outlined in her white skirt and apron, stared at them a little blankly before gesturing them into the house.

"Why don't you wait here?" she suggested, indicating with a dark and lovely upraised arm a large room to the left of the central hall.

By now even Hi was becoming a little jaded by all the rich interiors of the Clare College dependents, past and present. This room was almost as expensively decorated as Cornelius Vanderlyn's private museum. Of course, Hi and Tig could not have known it, but the people who inhabited this space were, in fact, the former neighbors of the Vanderlyns, and the woman of the house was that same Mrs. Hughes who had returned the young Cornelius's *Laocoön* to his mother after her own son had purloined it on that distant, snow-smothered day. The Hugheses and the Vanderlyns were, in the local hierarchy, exactly on a par, both figuring prominently in the interlaced histories of Westerly and Clare, and so a natural, though never overt, rivalry had developed between them, and they seemed at times to be imitating one another. For example, both had abandoned their large and expensive inherited properties at roughly the same period, moving into more compact and convenient lodgings in or near the campus. The house which Hi and Tig had entered seemed, like Professor Vanderlyn's apartment, to be bursting with treasures accumulated over many generations, each object redolent of memories and the money which pays for the illusion that we can retain them in tangible form.

The brother and sister walked into the drawing room, both moving by instinct to the fireplace, where a fire was burning, another proof that someone was home. Over the carved mantel hung an enormous picture, in fact, an unknown masterpiece by the English painter, John Everett Millais, executed during his pre-Raphaelite days. It was unknown only because it had been purchased directly from the artist by an ancestor of Professor Hughes in the eighteen-fifties and had never been exhibited outside of Westerly. The subject it depicted was an intriguing, if rather gruesome, one, identified by the title, *Last Rites in the Highlands*, inscribed on the lower border of the heavy gilt frame. The setting was a Scottish cemetery at evening, the time of day evinced by dark and billowing clouds outlined in the distance with a streak of lurid crimson. In the foreground, two kilted brothers with red beards and wild eyes were robbing a freshly-filled grave. The subject was more precisely explicated, and its particular horror brought home, by a Burnsian quatrain, quoted, in Gothic script, immediately below the title:

> For family luve, this pair car'd no' a
> fither—
> Ta' the grave they descended,
> The coffin upended,
> An' snatch'd the weddin' band frae their
> ain mither!

Hi was at once repulsed and delighted by the picture, a precocious example of the artist's mastery of narrative and detail. Both he and his sister remained studying it from below when a woman entered the room unheard, and, after a moment, greeted them cordially. This was Mrs. Hughes.

Amanda Clovis Carmichael Hughes was her own background. That is not to say that she was fat—she was decidedly overweight, but that was not why she seemed so territorial and diffuse. It was rather that her personality, which was even bigger than her actual person, filled a space, like foam insulation. She had always commanded attention; in her youth, as the eldest daughter of an old but faded Baltimore family, her cleverness and her expansive zeal had never failed to impress a growing circle of acquaintances, among whom she was an object of awe rather than admiration or affection. Now, just past seventy, she seemed a massive pink and powdered personification of age-old manners, a mountain of gentility rich with hidden mines of insight and vituperation, old prejudices and more modern, if less obviously feminine, ambitions. For, as everyone knew, she had been the key to the successful career of her husband, Armitage Quincy Hughes. Lax and arrogant by nature, that gentleman might have gone through his entire life without accomplishing anything, much less writing three books on the ancient Phoenicians (though the wicked envious insisted it was the same book three times over), content instead to play the role of the New England aristocrat, living off the Hughes money and the Quincy name. But his union with Amanda Carmichael had changed all of that.

They had been married for fifty years, the last forty-eight of which had been completely devoid of happiness. They stayed together, if that is the correct way to describe their prolonged physical proximity, because of who they were, and, more importantly, because of who they thought people thought they were. When they were younger, they had the children to think of, a brood of three bullying boys and an only daughter whose *hauteur* was legendary in Westerly, though it would be too large and thankless a task to provide instances of it here. When the children were grown and their parents no longer felt the need to set an example of upright family behavior for their less distinguished neighbors, the couple had remained together from a deep-seated, though never acknowledged, fear that they were unlikely to appeal to anyone else. And so their alliance had continued: she, with her constant criticism, spurring him on to ever greater positions of power at the college, and he, quietly accepting but resenting her interference, vengefully thwarting any claims she might make in the more private atmosphere of the home. The suffering they caused each other was a kind of glue; they used it profusely, and now, in their golden years, they would never come unstuck.

Naturally, none of this was immediately apparent to the two young professors. To them, Mrs. Hughes was a large, smiling lady whose outfit blended imperceptibly into the chintz upholstery on the English club chairs arranged in conversational groupings about the room. And when she spoke, her voice was like the last gasp of the antebellum South: delicate, artificial, and inevitably suspect.

"I am Amanda Hughes. My maid said you wanted to see me. Something to do with the college, I presume?"

If Hiawatha had been cowed by the straightforward warnings of Detective Staves, he was even more intimidated—and on a deeper, less conscious level—by the dulcet tinklings of Mrs. Hughes, which were like ripples of honey, concealing a sting. She was simply too large and absorbent-looking, her smile altogether too incongruous, not to be frightening. Even the more rational and courageous Tig felt herself in the presence of an unpredictable hazard. Nevertheless, she faced the situation she had brought about head on.

"Mrs. Hughes. It is so nice to meet you at last. I'm Antigone Musing, from the Department of Chemistry. My brother and I . . ."

Here Tig raised a hand to Hi, who bowed slightly, like a Chinese lackey.

" . . . have heard a great deal about you. I hope you won't think us outrageous, but we've come to talk to you about the Vanderlyn affair."

Whether it was Antigone's mention of the Vanderlyn name or her seemingly guileless use of the term "affair," Mrs. Hughes' reaction was immediate, if hardly detectible. It was as though a shadow passed swiftly over the colorless complexion of her face. The older woman seemed to be thinking fast. Finally, never changing her expression, she walked up to the large painting and said, with a distinct contraction of the drawl which had marked her greeting, "It's very difficult to look at such an image, under the circumstances. I wonder if we shouldn't take it down."

Then Mrs. Hughes turned again to the Musings and asked them to be seated. When all three had done so, their involuntary hostess began again.

"Well, what is your interest in the matter? Of course, my husband and I have already spoken to the police. Not in person; my husband has been a bit under the weather lately. But we both talked to a detective on the telephone. I'm afraid we were not very helpful."

Mrs. Hughes sitting seemed even larger and more formidable than Mrs. Hughes erect. And Hi felt that in this position she seemed an automatic and unquestionable center, drawing all threads to herself. Tig, on the other hand, never paused to consider Mrs. Hughes' counterparts in the insect world, so set was she on obtaining something new which might help her to help Cornelius Vanderlyn.

"The fact is, Mrs. Hughes, that my brother and I are here, against the admonitions of the police not to interfere, in order to see if there isn't some way we might help Professor Vanderlyn."

Hi knew well enough that his sister could be disarming and also that she was, far more than himself, what might be called "honest." But he had rarely seen her combine the two qualities so remarkably as now. He applauded her, in his head, and waited with her to see what Mrs. Hughes would say.

That woman seemed to be flipping through a variety of options for handling the awkward situation which, in the guise of these young strangers, had wormed its way, more effectively but also more irritatingly than had the police, into her living room. She had to think fast, but that was only one of her fortes. She weighed what the two intruders might already know. Her pride told her that, at the very least, they would assume more than an acquaintance existed between the Hugheses and the Vanderlyns, neck and neck as they had always been in Westerly society. Furthermore, her husband had been chairman of the Classics Department when Cornelius was hired. It was also possible that they had heard rumors of an affair between her husband and the late Mrs. Vanderlyn. The former was upstairs in his office, working at the computer on something obscure. Contrary to what she had been telling everyone, he was fitter than ever. It was lucky that Stellita knew her job well enough to bring all news of visitors directly to her mistress. Amanda considered briefly being perfectly honest. What difference, after all, could it make to anyone now if, twenty years ago, her husband had played for one night the Elder to Virginia Vanderlyn's Susannah? The suggestion that there was a Biblical precedent for either of them made her want to laugh, but she had long ago forgotten how. Instead, she felt a renewed and more familiar fury. Finally she chose her mode.

"Well, if anybody ever felt sorry for a person, I've felt sorry for Cornelius Vanderlyn. We used to live right next door to them, you know. My son, Harmon, was a great friend of his when they were growing up. Of course, even then I could tell there were problems. I mean, not everyone can be skilled in athletics, as my boys were, but Van never even tried. He was—how shall I put it?—a bit of a weakling. And if it isn't unfair, coming from an old friend of the family, he was also a bit . . . unusual. Still, that was more the fault of his parents. His father was all right, but his mother, I'm afraid, was more interested in her own academic pursuits than in running a home. If I sound like I'm gossiping, it's only because I, too, wish I could help the poor man."

Antigone and Hi were impressed by Mrs. Hughes' recital and even more by the fact that it was their own plain dealing that had elicited it. Neither wanted to disturb the momentum of her narrative, though after a pause, Hi risked a word of encouragement taken straight out of a courtroom drama.

"Please, do go on."

"Well, for some men, if they are at all weak or undirected, marriage can be a sort of salvation. A reason for living and striving. And the proper spouse can be a kind of human inspiration, and a standard, as well. If you see what I mean."

Here it was pretty clear that Mrs. Hughes was referring to herself and the role she had played in her own husband's life. She was also, Hi was sure, acting. At any moment he expected her to launch into a monologue on the intangible rewards of wifely virtue. Perhaps in ancient Phoenician. His eye wandered somewhat about the room, reluctant to catch her own. But the older woman was, at least figuratively speaking, reflected in every surface surrounding them.

"Cornelius's marriage was a tragedy. Yes, I use the word in its most shattering sense. He was a man who might have risen to greatness, despite even the neglect of his parents, but he was brought down by circumstances. My husband retired after a term as acting provost. I'm not saying that Cornelius could have aimed that high, but he had undeniable talents. His marriage laid them to rest once and for all. I would be dishonest if I didn't maintain now what I have been saying for years: Virginia Vanderlyn, whatever happened to her, brought it on herself. Oh, I know what people say, that Armitage was attracted to her and that I'm a vindictive old woman. But nothing could be further from the truth! Both my husband and I tried to be kind to them. Armitage gave Cornelius his first job, after all, and I did my best to introduce her to the other college wives. But she seemed ignorant of even the most basic principles of civilized behavior. We both saw through her soon enough. But Cornelius? She had that man in her power from the moment they met. If Cornelius killed her, she certainly drove him to it. If you ask me, her death was a kind of suicide."

With this speech, delivered under a sort of spell of conjugal fervency, Mrs. Hughes rose again, apparently to indicate that the three minutes she could spare them were up. Impossible now for Hiawatha or Antigone to remind the woman that the "suicide" she theorized for Virginia Vanderlyn also involved "self burial." Still, neither brother nor sister moved, unwilling to accept the interview as over. Antigone finally spoke up.

"But do you believe that Cornelius could have killed her?"

"Stellita!" Mrs. Hughes called, as a second sign that her guests must be leaving now. But she did make one last comment as they begrudgingly got up from the sofa.

"All I know is, when he was a child, he was forever burying things. Things he loved."

She said this as she conducted them to the front door. Then she seemed to shift roles all at once, speaking again in the more mellifluous tones with which she had greeted them.

"I wish I could have you stay longer. I'm naturally very interested in whatever happens to poor Cornelius. And the boy! But I'm afraid, with my husband unwell, and our own children due home any minute for the holidays . . . well, I'm sure you understand."

Very gently but firmly, Hi and Tig were expelled from the house. When the door was closed upon them, Mrs. Hughes turned to see her husband on the landing of the stairs.

"Who was that?" said Armitage Quincy Hughes, a very youthful and robust-looking seventy-three-year-old with a rower's build and wavy silver hair.

"Oh, just some curious colleagues wanting to know more about the Vanderlyns," replied Mrs. Hughes. "Don't worry, dear. I've protected you again." And as she spoke, her eyes glittered, but not protectively, rather like those of a creature who likes to take its time devouring its prey. Amanda Hughes had been eating this particular crow for twenty years.

Aloud, her husband replied, "Thank you. You're the best. The world doesn't deserve you."

He turned back up the stairs, adding, but not quite under his breath, "Now why don't you die, and prove the point?"

XIX

CORNELIUS VANDERLYN SAT IN THE SMALL DINING alcove adjacent to his disproportionately large kitchen, with its glass-doored cabinets containing stacks of old Spode plates and the better bits of the family silver. He was idly looping the last strands of spaghetti onto the end of his fork. Behind him, on a ceramic countertop, sat the neglected casserole that Judy Wagner Dumont had delivered less than an hour ago. Mrs. Dumont had, as always at this and other times of year, rung his bell unannounced, and despite the usual polite attempts of Professor Vanderlyn to keep her in the foyer, she had bustled past him—today she seemed almost to have dipped and scuttled between his legs—into the kitchen, talking all the time.

"Now I've got to warn you, Van," she said, laying a shopping bag half her size on the counter. "There's some weirdo running around, wearing a sort of disguise, and asking questions about you. Of course, I didn't tell him anything."

"What is there to tell?" Cornelius wondered aloud, watching her unload the bag.

Judy looked him in the eye, to accomplish which she had to look almost straight up.

"All I'm saying is, be careful."

"Who is this 'weirdo,' do you think?"

"He's a youngish man with blond hair and fake glasses. The weirdest part of all is that he calls himself Hiawatha!" Judy chortled, absolutely convinced this was an alias and a female one to boot.

At this description, Cornelius smiled broadly, but said nothing. He listened to Judy for fifteen minutes as she chattered on about her regrets that her husband had insisted on having his family come to her house for Thanksgiving the next day. Otherwise, she would so much like to have had Cornelius and Charlie. And she wanted to know how poor Charlie was, and to remind Cornelius to be sure and warn his son about the mysterious and fraudulent Hiawatha. When she was finally ready to go, she took the top off of the casserole she had made, revealing a brown substance varying in consistency from thin and gruel-like to stiff and lumpy. This she proudly identified as "Indian Summer Stew," adding that it was filled with nutritious ingredients. Of these, Cornelius was able to recognize only one or at most two—mushrooms from their shape and, it seemed, maple syrup from the smell. After he had thanked her and at last seen her off, he returned to the kitchen to cook some spaghetti. He didn't, at this moment, have the stomach even to dispose of the seasonal stew.

Now, at the end of his meal, he was once again feeling the panic of impending boredom. Nor did he have the usual distracting presence of his wife's ghost. In fact, over the past few days, she had become a less frequent companion, and though he could still conjure her up, Cornelius found that it was increasingly difficult to keep her there. Furthermore, when she did appear, on her own or at his summons, he noticed that she was less substantial each time. It was as though she was losing her opacity. In short, he was beginning to see through her.

After washing the plate and the pot which were the only dishes he had used to make his meal, he suddenly decided to act on an impulse that had recurred throughout the day. He reached for the telephone and dialed the number of his son Charlie's room at the dormitory. Though the odds were against his being home at this hour, someone did greet him at the other end of the line.

"Hello. That's not Charlie, is it?" asked his father.

"No, it's Michael Smith. Who is this?" asked the voice.

"This is Charlie's father. Hello, Michael. I'm calling to be sure that you're both coming to dinner tomorrow. I also wanted to tell Charlie that I'm going to invite a couple of my colleagues, as well. Is Charlie there?"

"No, he's not here right now. He's taking a shower. But I can tell him to call you right back. And I'm very grateful that you've asked me to dinner tomorrow. If my parents weren't out of the country, of course, I would go home, but . . ."

"That's fine. We're happy to have you. And tell Charlie when he comes back that I'm asking Professor Musing and her brother to come, too. I think he should be glad to hear it. I know how much he likes Professor Musing."

"Will do," responded Michael Smith before hanging up the receiver.

Cornelius did the same, and then, after obtaining it from the operator, dialed the number for Antigone Musing.

Antigone and Hiawatha were busily packing, Hi more anxiously, but less eagerly, than his sister.

Though they were in different rooms, they continued to carry on a conversation by yelling back and forth. Hi was in the middle of reiterating his astonishment at the willingness of Mrs. Hughes to talk to them, when the telephone rang, and he followed his sister—at a safe distance, for answering the telephone was among his top ten aversions—into the living room, where she picked it up.

"Oh, hello, Professor Vanderlyn. Yes, I'm sorry, Cornelius."

"The Minotaur himself!" Hi half-shouted, before his sister shushed him with a serious look.

"No, you're not disturbing us at all. No, we're not in the middle of being burgled. That's just my brother making noise in the background. . . . Yes, of course, I'd love to have come. The fact is we've already promised our parents that we would be with them. . . . No, I wish it had worked out. . . . Yes, we may be back by Saturday night. . . . Of course, I look forward to seeing you there. No, believe me, the loss is ours. . . . Thank you so much for thinking of us."

As Antigone replaced the receiver, she felt suddenly solemn and more than a little disappointed. Cornelius had asked her and her brother to come for Thanksgiving dinner, and although it had been Tig who had been pushing her brother to agree to go home, now she wished that she had pushed less hard.

After all, they could go home in a few weeks for Christmas, and their parents wouldn't be any worse off. They had their other children, Flannery and Jane, whereas Cornelius would be practically alone. But she had to face the fact that even if he were hosting a dinner for sixty, with a small orchestra, she would have wanted to be among his guests. And perhaps to sit next to him. The holidays are a terrible time when it comes to awakening desire.

Some of this she related to Hi, and what she left out, she knew he could infer, as they returned to their packing. Thankfully, with his own worries about seeing his family for the first time in a year, and after avoiding them so pointedly, he was not interested in teasing Tig about her romantic inclinations. But the telephone call had helped her to decide to come back for Randall Ross's party on Saturday night. She would see Cornelius there, and maybe she would feel sufficiently confident, after the success of returning home with the prodigal Hi, to risk letting her attraction be known.

In his bedroom, Hi stared down at the gaping old leather case and wondered how his clothes had managed to expand so since his arrival less than a week ago. But he was at least as aware as his sister that this was only one more manifestation of his desire to avoid the imminent Thanksgiving feast with his family. He considered briefly how he might make the best of the situation. For example, he could forget to pack altogether, thereby allowing, if not actually forcing, his parents to indulge him with the money for some new clothes. Then, in the evening, when his father turned on him—for Hiawatha knew that this was bound to happen—and they fought, and Hiawatha stormed out—for good, this time—he would at least have an outfit to show for his suffering. But what about his mother's suffering? There was the old dilemma, and even his inability to resolve it helped him to fill the suitcase, which he did as though in a trance, thinking that, at any rate, it would be good to have a few things to wear, in case it all went better this time.

Cornelius stared at the dining table, and was almost relieved that the Musings would not be able to come, for even if he could find the leaf, it wouldn't sit more than four very comfortably.

SOME RIDDLES, AND A PARABLE
(PRELIMINARY TO THE NEXT CHAPTER)

Where have we all been and can never leave?

What, like bread,
Grows before it is finished,
And its goal is to be diminished?

What gets bigger as we go backward in time?

What is a myth in which all of the characters are real?

What is like gold, among our most precious resources?
Like silver, often pays our way? And, like lead,
weighty enough to impede our progress?

What is as different as we are, but also, inevitably, the
same?

What lies to us, about us, and, above all, for us?

What, like water, rocks us? Like air, surrounds us?
Like fire, often flares up? And, like the earth, we cannot avoid coming back to?

What can we never lose, nor ever control?

What rides us, hounds us, guides us, is brought low when we fall, and helps us up again?

What is ours, that is also ourselves?

The answer to all these riddles is our families.

And now for the parable:

If the kingdom of heaven is like a mustard seed, then our families, or better still, "each person's family," is like the young man who made a wish. The next day, he woke to discover his pillowcase filled with gold. Taking his newfound fortune, he set off for England to buy himself some clothes. But on the way, his boat encountered a storm and was driven to the west coast of Africa. There, the young man, like certain characters in similar circumstances in Voltaire's *Candide*, was captured by pirates, imprisoned, and eventually made a slave. After ten years of painful labor in the galleys, he was set free, due to the intervention of the pirate captain's wife, who had fallen in love with him. The two ran off together, but she died shortly thereafter. In her will, she left the young man her entire fortune. Falling among brigands, he was only just barely able to buy his way out of certain re-enslavement and back to the West, where he landed, after another journey by water, in France. There at last he met and married a beautiful French dancer, and they lived quite happily together to an august old age. This, of course, had been the original object of the young man's wish—that is, he had not asked for money, nor adventure, but to marry and live out his life with a beautiful woman.

The family is like this young man in many ways. Both start off with little more than wishes, and even those are invariably based on appetites and received ideas. Both spend much of their time at sea, and only rarely are their movements the results of their intentions. Both are subject to violence, and repeated submission, and both react with a moral system based not on ideals, but upon survival. But the family is like the young man above in all this: its disappointments, inconceivable until they occur, are essential to the fulfillment of its dreams. Its happiness is inseparable from its misfortune, and both, however unmerited, make up its only true legacy, the will of the story itself to live on after, and in spite of, the death of the characters.

XX

OPENING THE DOOR OF HIS BEDROOM IN HIS parents' house, an old light flooded the dark cell of Hiawatha's heart. And what did that light illuminate, what pleasures of a distant past, abandoned long ago like toys outgrown, that still beckoned to be retrieved or only touched once more, and made to exist by the familiar human contact that is their completion? What wrongs, committed or borne, what doubts and disappointments, what catastrophic episodes now buried, like ill-obtained treasures or the insect victims of childhood crimes, under the floorboards, that nevertheless could not be still because they were never entirely forgotten, nor ever redressed?

What hosts of passion, unbounded hatreds and blood-cursing jealousies but even more numerous loves, yes, above all, the loves both logical and illogical that surpassed, in depth and duration, all other passions spent or conceived in that cell, that danced like motes and were only just barely still real, but real?

Hiawatha placed his suitcase gently on the single bed and faced the fact that he had broken his vow again. He had promised himself, and not only himself, but his one or two good friends who had extracted the promise, that he would not return home before he was ready. And he had to acknowledge what came to him with some impact right now: he was not ready.

Hi's room was on the third, topmost floor of his parents' house, which was one in a row of many squat, brick-fronted dwellings that seemed larger than they were due to the narrowness of the street they faced, a former mews in Boston's North End. His father had purchased the property thirty years before, when the neighborhood was ripe for renovation, and the family had grown as their surroundings were transformed. Now the area was fashionable and expensive, a genteel residential core bounded by coffee shops, florists, and antiqueries, all within hearing of the bells of the Old North Church and Bulfinch's Saint Stephen's.

The sound of these bells was hardly noticed by Hi, who slowly unpacked his things and vaguely listened for noises from the two floors below. He thought he could hear Tig moving around in the bedroom immediately beneath his, which she had shared with their younger sister, Jane. Because both Jane and their older sister, Flannery, were married and lived near Boston, Tig would have her old room to herself on this visit. An unmarried uncle, whom the younger generation of Musings affectionately referred to as Uncle Synonym, would be staying in Flannery's former bedroom, opposite Hi's. And diagonally underneath Hiawatha was the suite his parents occupied. Hiawatha focused his ears in that direction and on the first floor rooms of the house, anxious to determine if his parents, who had been out shopping when Hi and Tig arrived, had returned. As yet, there was no sign, and so, until someone summoned him and insisted upon his descent, he lay down on the bed, leaving his shoes on but keeping his feet at an angle and off the old quilt.

Tig, too, enacted the rituals of the returning, emptying the few things she had brought in her suitcase into her old dresser. Again she was forced to consider the irony that she had fought hard to get Hi home, and now all she could think about was Cornelius, back at Clare, perhaps accompanied by Charlie, though of this she could not be sure. She pictured her new friend sitting in his strange museum, surrounded but not distracted by images and fragments

of a past which predated his own. She was looking
forward to seeing her parents and siblings, but she
was even more anxious to take Hi back with her on
Saturday, to see Cornelius at Randall Ross's party.
After, of course, the successful accomplishment of
this reunion. She paused in her unpacking to listen
for Hiawatha upstairs in his room under the eaves,
and when she heard nothing, she lay down for a brief
nap on her bed.

Downstairs in the dining room, with its 1920's
reproduction colonial furniture, the table was already
set. It had, in fact, been set for days, according to a
habit of Mrs. Musing's, which never failed to provoke
the same critical comments from her husband and
forced her to dust the dishes lightly on the actual day
of the meal. Mr. Musing, being a man and every bit as
old-fashioned as the furniture, could not grasp that his
wife was equally fond of her dishes—a set of fine
Bavarian porcelain in a shade of palest sage, against
which gorgeous damask roses dilated to bursting—
and of seeing them arranged and ready for family use.
It was only at the holidays that she indulged in displaying her nicest things, and most of her nicest
things pertained to eating; thus, the formal eating
room, forgotten for most of the year, became, for a few
weeks, the dazzling centerpiece of the whole place,
like the combination bedroom-death chamber of King

Sardanapalus in the famous picture by Delacroix. Not that Mrs. Musing's tastes were the least bit Assyrian. The overall effect she sought was that achieved by the American period rooms which were her favorite part of any museum, though she recognized that her own dining room was a conflation of many periods. But this, she argued mentally, was only one source of its superiority. Because the room faced south, it was well-lit and warm.

And into this room, at half past five, streamed all the people who truly mattered to Mrs. Musing. Taking their places at table were the eldest daughter, Flannery, a successful financial advisor at one of the largest brokerage firms in New England, and her husband, Roger, an only slightly less successful financial advisor at one of the only slightly smaller brokerage firms in the same region. Flannery and Roger had met as students in business school, and since then, they had rarely been out of one another's sight. Their two children, Arthur and Sylvie, were also present. Both were in their mid-teens, and they detested each other. Their parents never interfered with the children's frequent expressions, verbal and physical, of their mutual contempt, insisting that it was only a natural phase they were going through, and so everyone politely refrained from making the observation that this particular phase had endured since the birth of the younger child. Sylvie, the elder, had recently been arrested for shoplifting, another phase in which the parents seemed almost to take pride.

Across from Flannery sat the youngest daughter, Jane. She was of a vivacious temperament, and her clothes cost more than all the outfits of everyone else in the room combined. This was perhaps one reason for her vivacity. She sat next to, and occasionally nudged, her husband, Dan, to whom she had been married for two years, but with whom she had been living for many more. Dan, an art dealer from a wealthy Cohasset family, had supported Jane for the six years it had taken her to obtain her degree in interior design. Theirs was a more publicly affectionate rapport than the no doubt deeper but less obviously physical bond between Flannery and Roger. Jane kept cooing into Dan's ear and making racy comments, sometimes accompanying them with ambiguous gestures. She was very clever and kept everybody giggling, though Mrs. Musing's giggle was perhaps less comfortable than those of the others.

Flanking Mrs. Musing at one end of the table sat her two unmarried children, Hiawatha and Antigone. Upon returning home from her last-minute shopping earlier in the day, Mrs. Musing had rushed as fast as her sixty-two-year-old legs would carry her up to the second floor, where she lavished affectionate hugs on

Antigone. In his bed on the floor above, Hiawatha was roused by the commotion, sat up, and waited. Sure enough, moments later, his mother and his sister arrived at his door, not pausing to knock, but charging in, his mother embracing him with enough force to break his spine, which made Hi very happy, after all. Because she didn't see them as often as she did her other children and their families, Mrs. Musing had selfishly seated Hi and Tig next to her, an arrangement no one seemed to mind.

At the opposite end of the table, Mr. Musing, in his habitual, dark blue cardigan, carved the turkey. And at his left was his unmarried brother, who was speaking now.

"What I can't under—er, comprehend—is why nobody took the trou—er, bothered to talk to—consult with—me. After all, I'm the woman's primary doct—physician."

Uncle Synonym, whose real name was Andrew, was a general practitioner who lived and worked in Sudbury. At sixty-three, he was only a year younger than Mr. Musing. He had a very kind face, and hair the unmodulated blackness of which suggested consistent dyeing.

Hiawatha, who was doing his best to be outgoing and yet knew that the success of this meal from his own point of view depended upon keeping the conversation on an impersonal level, responded.

"Well, at least they got her the liver. I mean, it couldn't have been kept waiting too long. Am I right?"

Mr. Musing, for the first time since his son had arrived home, looked directly at him, but said nothing, opting instead for a large swallow of wine.

Uncle Synonym, too, took a drink, before replying with a strange mixture of sadness and triumph.

"Yes, I agree. But of course, a few weeks later she gave it up—rejected it, and . . . died." His final word on that particular patient came as something of a surprise. Apparently, for those in the medical profession, unlike those outside of it, there are no synonyms for death.

Mrs. Musing, having listened to her brother-in-law's description of this poor woman's demise, after a respectful pause, spoke up brightly.

"Well, let's all concentrate on positive things now, shall we? For example, Flannery tells me that the stock market is booming. And Jane is working on her first decoration project for Dan's parents. And I want to hear all about Hiawatha's talk at Clare. Antigone tells me it went wonderfully."

"Yeah, except at the end, when a murdered woman's son burst into the room looking for Tig." Hi

said this in rather a lighthearted, ironical spirit, helping himself to mashed potatoes and then looking
around for the gravy.

Of course, everybody at the table had heard of the
recent events in Westerly, and even Mrs. Musing was
curious enough to include the topic of the Vanderlyns
in her designation of "positive things." None of the
others knew yet, however, how close to the situation
Hi and Tig had become.

"What is going on in that old college town?" asked
Flannery, with just a *soupçon* of condescension in her
voice. Clearly, whoever turned out to be guilty of mur-
dering the professor's wife, there was no money to be
made from the crime.

"Tell us, Tig," piped up Jane, simultaneously
pinching her husband's upper thigh under the table.

The latter gave a little jump, and then he, too,
asked for more information.

"Did you meet the guy, Hi? The son, I mean."

"Well, he's Tig's student. You start, Tig," Hi said
to his sister. Mrs. Musing turned from one to the
other as they spoke. Mr. Musing poured himself a
third glass of wine, his face a blend of bland emotions,
most visible among them being indifference. But
everyone was relatively quiet while Hi and Tig took
turns filling in the family on the only news story worthy of the name to come out of Westerly in years.

Occasionally one of the listeners interjected, Mrs. Musing with a "Really? No!" and Mr. Musing with a grunt or guffaw, Flannery with a comment on the dwindling portfolios of the New York Vanderlyns, and Jane with an inquiry as to exactly how well Tig knew the Hughes family, in case they ever needed to redecorate their home.

Recounting their experiences over the past week proved as diverting for Hi and Tig as it was for their listeners. At the moment when Tig was telling them all about the disguise that Hi had adopted to pay his visit to Judy Wagner Dumont, when Hi himself was feeling more relaxed in this environment than he had felt in years, Mr. Musing finally spoke.

"I'm afraid I don't understand how Hiawatha could find the time to be running around in false glasses," Hi's father remarked, with both arms on the table, joined around the glass in his hands.

"It seems—er, appears—to me that the whole thing was a kind of adven—caper," intoned Uncle Synonym, sympathetically.

Hi, whose face was flushed from the excitement of reliving his recent experiences, either did not, or consciously chose not to, notice the tone of criticism in his father's voice, instead responding to his uncle.

"Oh, it certainly was that!" And he smiled broadly at Tig.

"But," his father continued, "why weren't you back in Chicago? I assumed that you were taking time off in order to do some research, the sort of research one could hardly accomplish in the archives of the institution where you are employed."

Hi could not ignore the criticism now, but he did not respond.

Tig, as usual in these circumstances, spoke for him.

"Dad, I've already told you. Hi was staying with me so that we could come home together."

Their father took this as a challenge. Though he had been drinking, he was not the least bit intoxicated, or at least, his voice betrayed no alteration of his characteristic serious and clear-sighted manner.

"Tig, as I've told you before, you do no service to your brother by encouraging him in his idleness. Not that I'm not glad he's come home. But I am curious as to why he decided to stop punishing his mother and myself, after almost a year of ignoring us altogether. Hi?" His father said this undramatically, but he was definitely waiting for an answer.

A long pause followed, which Flannery finally ended.

"It wasn't very nice of you, Hi," she said, her tone at odds with her smiling features. While she was normally most jealous of the relationship between her father and the youngest daughter, Jane, she was always happy to expend a little energy keeping the other siblings down.

"Now, let's not ruin the evening by making accusations," Mrs. Musing began, but this was immediately taken as a further provocation by her husband.

"Do you mean to say that after eleven months of anxiety, during which time a day didn't go by without your telling me how worried you were about your precious boy, you're going to deny it all now?" Mr. Musing's voice was rising perceptibly. He put his glass down on the table with enough force to send a bit of wine splashing over the rim onto the cloth. Mrs. Musing saw this, but said nothing. Mr. Musing turned to Hi, and proceeded, over Antigone's attempt to interrupt.

"But it doesn't matter whether or not you punish us. What bothers me is that you continue making a mess of your life. You seem content to waste time at a second-rate school, you haven't produced anything since you finished your dissertation, and that, as you've admitted to me, was a weak effort, at best. You've made no progress in your personal life that I can see. You bounce from one therapist to another and vaguely hint at sexual confusion, something in which your mother may take an interest, but I do not. Is this all meant to be part of the punishment?"

Hi, staring down at his fingers, seemed to shift in slow motion to face his father.

"Speaking of punishment, do you know what I was thinking when I first got home today? I was thinking, there isn't a room in this house in which you haven't hit me." Hi's own voice was sinking as his father's rose.

This theme of abuse was a longstanding one between the two men, and bringing it up now was clearly calculated to exasperate the older Musing. Twenty years ago, when Hi was a boy, nobody talked about abuse the way they do today. And besides, Hiawatha had not been abused, physically, though he had been hit regularly. His father had tried to raise him the way he himself had been raised, strictly and without sentiment. And his father felt, above all, that raising a boy was different, and frankly more important, than raising girls. The girls had been treated gingerly, though with an indifference that was every bit as prejudicial and had equally far-reaching effects. But Hiawatha had received the brunt of his father's pent-up urge to exercise his will on an impressionable creature, his intense *need* to raise. To borrow an old analogy, Mr. Musing was like a gardener, in whose lesser beds a certain amount of untrained vegetation (the girls) was tolerated, but whose masterpiece was to be an espaliered pear tree the likes of which the world had never seen.

Hiawatha was that pear tree. His progress had not, however, answered to the gardener's pruning. With every blow as with a brutal twisting of the shears, with every denial of affection as with a torturous wiring to the wall, the plant had taken an unanticipated course, so that now all that could be said of the pattern of its growth is that it drooped a little even in sunlight, which it avoided as furtively as it did the dark.

Mr. Musing took a deep breath, before responding to his son's recriminations.

"It looks as though you're still in need of some sort of discipline. It's no wonder you can't keep a girl-friend. There's nothing to you. What a waste." These last words seemed to cost him as much as they were meant to cost the person to whom they were addressed. And then he took an enormous swallow of wine, before rising up from the table and looking down at Hi with renewed disgust.

"Girlfriends?" Hi chuckled hollowly. "As if I haven't known too many women!" And then looking straight into his father's face, an act of defiance he only rarely risked, he added, "And no kind men."

Hi's father picked up his wine glass and the half-empty bottle from the table. "Nice of you to pay us a visit," he said at last, before slowly leaving the room.

Throughout this frigid exchange, everyone, including Mrs. Musing, had remained silent. Hi's

mother had learned from long and hard experience
that her interference between the two males only
made her husband angrier and her son more ashamed.
And so when Hi turned to his mother, it was not to
reproach her, but to indicate, with the briefest look,
his sympathy for her. She was, for him, the personification of goodness, but she also confirmed his pes-
simistic conviction that good is ultimately ineffectual.

This silence continued for several moments after
the departure of Mr. Musing for his study or his bed.
Hi was staring blankly at his own fingers. Tig's heart
was pounding; though there was nothing in her life
that recurred with such predictable frequency, these
conversations never ceased to tear her apart. The
other siblings exchanged knowing looks. Finally, Mrs.
Musing spoke in a half-whisper.

"I just don't know what gets into him," she said,
like a woman for whom not solving an age-old problem has become habitual, but no less frustrating.

"He drinks too much," suggested Tig firmly.

"But it wasn't right that Hi didn't call home for so
long," the oldest sister hastened to inject. "Hi, why do
you have to upset him like that?"

Flannery shared her father's anxieties about Hi's
lack of ambition, his content to live in the Midwest
and above all the questionable sexual proclivities suggested by his prolonged bachelorhood. Added to

which, she wanted to keep the attention focused on her brother and off of her own children. The latter, seated on either side of their mother, had actually been enthralled and uncharacteristically quiet during the second half of the meal, and she hated to rob them of an entertainment that distracted them from their own internecine struggles, however natural those might be.

Roger looked skeptically at his wife, then rolled his eyes. Uncle Synonym started to speak, but thought that silence, after all, might prove the best substitute for a comment. Mrs. Musing sighed. Tig reached a hand towards Hi, who gently pushed it away. Dan gave Jane a reciprocal poke in her ribs, which caused that young woman to laugh loudly and enthusiastically, a laugh that, though her husband wouldn't recognize it, was a leftover from her traumatized, anorexic, high school days.

XXI

O N THE LAST TRAIN LEAVING BOSTON IN THE direction of Westerly, Hi sat alone, rigid as a sphinx, with his hand in his pocket and Tig's spare key in his hand. Despite his firm resolution not to dwell on the events of the evening which had resulted in his premature departure and his consequent feelings of uncertainty and embarrassment, emotions he was only barely able to prevent devolving into fury and shame (respectively), he nevertheless found himself re-enacting the awful dinner conversation over and over in his mind. And with each new version, the script changed slightly, so that before stopping in South Deerfield, his father had acquired a wicked, snarling laugh, and by the time they reached the heart of the Berkshires, Hi was reduced to a non-speaking role, one in which he merely greeted with a beatific smile each fresh arrow that tore through his tender hide.

Not that Hiawatha would have chosen the role of martyr if options had presented themselves. To be fair, the scene as it developed was not at all what he had pictured before making his overly hasty decision to let Tig take him home. What he had dreamed of, this time and often in the past, was more along the lines of the moving reunion illustrated by Rembrandt in his *Return of the Prodigal Son*: Hi, with shaven head and ragged shoes, kneeling before an octogenarian, all-forgiving papa, the pair of them surrounded by onlookers whose presence is less tangible than the darkness immersing them all. Of course, in that masterpiece, the father seems to have almost no alternative to the reconciliation, enfeebled as he is with age, which was hardly the case with Hiawatha's father, a man still youthfully alert and opinionated and hardly enfeebled at all by a slight tipsiness. Furthermore, because his head is hidden, the son's emotions are hard, if not impossible, to know. As always, Hiawatha's visions were baroque, broadly painted, and comfortably vague, and this precaution was, no doubt, one of the reasons for his perennial disappointment, as well.

Still, he could not but wince at the recollection of his mother's face when he said good-bye, with Tig immediately behind them in the front hall, finally giving up the fight to stop her brother from running away again. There are moments in every drama, however small, however common, when, coincidentally or due to some greater, authorial will, all the characters share the same knowledge. The hero is dead, the wedding is off, the culprit is revealed. The knowledge that Hiawatha would not stay the night in his parents' house—unwished for, if truth be told, even by his father, but especially contrary to the hopes of his mother and his one interested sister—was inescapably clear. Everyone knew better than to try to subvert the fact. Things could only get worse.

And so Hiawatha feverishly and familiarly tried to edit the recent footage of his life. But as the train rolled on toward the northwest corner of the state, he fell into a deep, dreamless sleep such as we are sometimes granted when we least expect or seem to have earned it. And while he slept, back in Westerly, another drama was unfolding its spiky red petals like the seasonal poinsettia. As the carillon at the center of the Clare campus struck one a.m., its echoes bounded off the walls of the nearby college buildings, emptier than usual because most of the students had left for the holiday. Only one young man remained outdoors at this hour, and, despite his proximity, he was less likely than anyone to hear the sound of the bells, lying, as he was, at the base of the clock tower.

Was he drunk? Had he lost or eluded his fellow revelers? But his fellow revelers had been few. In fact, he had dined with a professor and the professor's son, who was his friend. And they had not gotten drunk, though the wine had been good. No, for the boy known as Michael Smith, there had been nothing like overindulgence this evening. There had been a simple, traditional meal, followed by a little television back in Charlie Vanderlyn's dormitory room. Then the two young men had said good-night. Michael had ostensibly headed back to his own room, though nobody except Charlie knew where that was. And Michael had made a brief detour, which had ended up being a definitive one. For he would remain at the base of the clock tower till early next morning, when a scream would bring the college security, who would call in the local police, who would have him carried away.

XXII

WELL I THINK YOUR LITTLE COLLEAGUE, ANTIGONE or Electra or whatever she calls herself, is taking on airs lately. She's not even tenured! And that weird brother of hers is even worse."

Bonnie Schtek offered this comment, in the unlikely combination of a whisper and a roar, to her husband, Hans. They were standing in one corner of Randall Ross's living room, each balancing a martini glass and a little paper plate loaded with hors d'oeuvres.

Hans's colleague, Antigone, had just arrived at the party, with her brother, Hiawatha; they had both been received with exceptional warmth by the always amiable Professor Ross, who took their coats and escorted them toward the sideboard to make their drinks. The living and dining rooms of the house were filling up fast, each new arrival extending the perimeter of what formed the large circle of Randall Ross's friends and acquaintances.

From the corner opposite that occupied by the Schteks came the shrill, invidious voice of Lucy Elevenish, who was loudly bemoaning the unmitigated brightness of New England skies, so inferior to those of her beloved London, from which, she claimed—wistfully but untruthfully—this semester in Westerly had been her longest separation.

As Hiawatha raised the glass of champagne to his lips, he reflected with some surprise that he was actually glad to be back in this room, surrounded by strangers, as he had been only a week ago following his talk. Since his solitary return to Westerly late Thursday night, he had done little but watch television in his pajamas on his sister's couch, ordering pizza and neglecting to shave. But now he was happy to be out again, and the impersonality of the crowded room, the lack of intimate ties between himself and the other guests, relaxed and pleased him.

Hiawatha was sufficiently wrapped up in his own thoughts not to notice his host's enraptured glance resting on the one person in the room with whom Hi did have an intimate relationship, namely, his sister. Antigone, too, was sipping champagne, and while Professor Ross studied her discreetly, she scanned the growing clusters of guests, looking for Cornelius Vanderlyn. Like her brother, she was remarkably happy to be here. For the past two days she had felt confused and frustrated, her emotions divided unequally between family-induced anxiety and an occasional rush of elation at the prospect of seeing Cornelius again. She had spent the entire day after Thanksgiving shopping with, and consoling, her mother. She had even managed, later that evening, to re-establish relations with her father. As Mr. Musing was deeply proud of his middle daughter and as he was already fighting a perennial, but never acknowledged, guilt about his treatment of his son, he was content and even eager to accept her unspoken apology for interfering with his patrician duties. By the end of their Friday dinner, he was no longer cross, being once again in his cups and able to imagine Hi, without allies, emotionally starved-out and eventually forced to return to the family on his father's terms. Antigone drove back to Westerly early the following day.

Now she stood next to her brother, unaware of Ross's admiring scrutiny of her across the sideboard as he distractedly fixed a drink for another guest.

This turned out to be a foreigner, a large, effeminate, middle-aged man who was staying with the Rosses over the holiday. Partly out of instinctive politeness, but also in order to prolong his time near Antigone, Ross brought the man to meet his two younger friends. The older man's name was Signor Marco Cavalizza; he spoke excellent English, and in that tongue he proclaimed both his origin and his orientation.

"Well, I am from Torino, in the north of Italy. You call it Turin. Do you know it? I live there with my partnair, Giorgio, who teaches at the university, in pheesics. I myself no longer teach, having been left sufficiently weel off by my parents not to need to adapt my scholastic views to the tyranny of the academia."

Hi and Tig exchanged a quick look before Hi responded pleasantly.

"And what brings you here? A love of turkey and cranberry sauce? And how do you know the Rosses?"

Signor Cavalizza slowly and deliberately sipped his vermouth. After a pause, during which he seemed to be mentally assessing the quality of the beverage, he addressed the Musings.

"I was veesiting New York, to celebrate the publication of my new book, or rather, the book for which I wrote an introduction. It is a catalogue of the great Italian conceptual artist, Gino Pupuzzeri. Do you know his work? No doubt you have seen photographs of the famous *Animal Feces* he produced for the 1972 *Biennale di Venezia?*"

Hi allowed Antigone to field this one.

"No, I'm afraid I'm dreadfully out of touch when it comes to contemporary art," said Tig, trying to appear interested but wishing desperately that Cornelius would come and take her and her brother away.

Without seeming to register her response, Signor Cavalizza continued his recital.

"As far as your question about the food, I love turkey, but I loathe the cranberry sawze of which you speak. It is disgusting."

This from a man who writes about animal poo, thought Hi and Tig, without speaking.

After another swallow of vermouth and another little pause, Cavalizza finally finished his reply to the three questions Hiawatha had already forgotten.

"As for the Rosses, I have known Randall and Laura for many years, since they came to stay with me and my partnair, Giorgio, in Torino, during a conference. That was when I still taught at the institute there. It must be seex years ago."

While the Italian was still talking, Hi and Tig were distracted by the voice of Randall Ross, who had been engaged in a new conversation with someone unknown to either of them. They were discussing details of the recent tragedy of Michael Smith, the poor boy found dead at the base of the college clock tower on the morning after Thanksgiving. Hi had seen a small picture of the boy in the local newspaper just this morning, but he had not recognized him, though the name was familiar. When Antigone heard the name, however, she wheeled around, and, completely forgetting their new acquaintance from Turin, asked Ross to tell her what had happened.

"It's terribly sad," Professor Ross began reluctantly. "A suicide, it seems. The kid had eaten dinner at Cornelius Vanderlyn's, of all places. Poor Van, he's really had his share lately. Of course, I was hoping he'd come to the party tonight, but he called to say he didn't see how he could. Apparently this Michael Smith, who killed himself, was his son's best friend. But he's not the first kid to jump from a window during the holidays. From what I hear, his parents were in Europe."

"Hi," gasped Antigone, "that's the kid who came to take Charlie away after your talk!"

"I thought his name sounded familiar, Tig. But you haven't been back long enough for us to talk about it."

Antigone paused retroactively to consider the disappointing news that Cornelius wouldn't be among the guests this evening. Then she turned back to Randall Ross.

"Suicide? Are they sure? How do they know?" Her thoughts were racing again. It was awfully coincidental and, frankly, looked bad for Cornelius, who was beginning to take on a fatal aura. The man to whom Ross had been speaking interrupted at this point.

"But that's just it! They don't know that it was suicide at all. In fact, they don't even know who the kid was. Everyone just assumed that he was a student here at Clare, but it turns out that there is NO Michael Smith enrolled at Clare nor living in any accommodation affiliated with the college. At least, that's what my wife was telling me. It's all very suspicious."

Antigone and Hiawatha were, to put it mildly, enthralled, and fixed their attention on this new font of information, who turned out to be a young colleague of Randall Ross's in the English department by the name of Fred Nolan. Professor Nolan's wife was a freelance journalist with connections at the local police department, and she was the ultimate source of these details concerning the death of the young man believed, though not proved, to be Michael Smith.

"But who was the poor kid, if he wasn't a student?" asked Hi, confident that Antigone would make no reference to his own attempts at freelance journalism.

"No one has any idea. He had a fake student ID card with the name Michael Smith, but he also had what seems to be a real New York driver's license with some other name. I can't remember it right this minute, but there was a Manhattan address on it. The police are looking into it now. But if he wasn't a student, why was he here? And, more intriguing still, why would he kill himself by jumping off the Clare clock tower?"

"And how did he even get into the clock tower at that time of night?" asked Tig.

"And especially on that night?" added Hi.

At this point, Signor Cavalizza, who seemed anxious to enter the conversation, spoke up.

"Yes, and that was the same night that we had some trouble here at the Rosses'."

"What kind of trouble?" Hi and Tig spoke simultaneously, the former turning to the Italian and the latter turning to Randall Ross.

"It was nothing. Some drunk tried to break into our basement. Nothing happened. The lock on the cellar door was broken, but whoever it was got away." Ross seemed entirely unconcerned about the attempted entry.

"Did you call the police?" Tig wanted to know.

"There wasn't any reason to call the police," answered a woman's voice very calmly. Everyone turned to see Laura Ross, who had come upon the conversation from another part of the room. She looked pale and lovely, if a bit tired, in a loose-fitting claret dress with very simple lines. She was carrying a plate of hot little cheese-filled things, which she handed to her husband. Hiawatha, Antigone, and Professor Nolan all greeted her warmly, after which she added, "In fact, I think that cellar door's been broken for ages."

"But I heard the noise," interjected Mr. Cavalizza. "A scratching noise at first, exactly like I heard the time when my partnair, Giorgio, and I were burglared in Torino." He raised his eyebrows to signal that he understood the suspense he had caused before concluding, "No, don't worry, none of the art was stolen."

Before the discussion could proceed, there was a slight commotion in the direction of the front door of the house. And when Antigone turned with the others to see what was happening, she was confronted by Cornelius Vanderlyn, advancing quickly in the direction of the little group stationed near the sideboard. Tig's immediate reaction was one of gladness, though, like Hiawatha and the rest of the group, she was surprised to see him here. And as he approached, their surprise increased. Cornelius looked—what one would formerly have thought it impossible for him to look—wild and disheveled. His fine silver hair was uncombed, his brows contracted, and beneath them, his eyes were wide and bloodshot. When he reached the small circle of holiday acquaintances, he spoke loudly and quickly to Randall Ross, hardly seeming to notice the others, which caused Tig, especially, some concern.

"Randall, I'm so sorry, but I've got to talk to you. The police are no help at all. It's Charlie. He's disappeared. Disappeared!"

Several other guests at the party were now looking to see what was going on. A number of them recognized Cornelius and were dying of curiosity to know what had happened. Randall Ross hastened to action. He grabbed Cornelius by the arm and led him upstairs to a bedroom where they could have some privacy. Instinctively, Antigone and Hiawatha followed them. Laura stayed behind, reassuring the bewildered guests that there was nothing at all wrong. The eyes of the hefty aesthete from Torino bulged with interest, noting and seeming to gather up the reactions of as many people around him as possible.

Upstairs, Randall Ross ushered Cornelius, Hi, and Tig into a large bedroom with a great canopied four-poster and an enormous chest of drawers. He closed the door behind them, and then he sat down on the edge of the bed. Cornelius was actually panting, and Antigone trembled for him. In recognition of her empathy, Cornelius looked at her briefly and nodded without saying a word. Hiawatha, whose sympathies over the past two days had been reserved exclusively for himself, was happy now to split them between his sister and their new friend. Remaining perfectly calm, Professor Ross revealed himself at once the master of the situation.

"Now Van, tell us again exactly what's happened," he began.

Cornelius took a deep breath, but seemed altogether uncertain as to where he should begin.

"Charlie and I spent the entire morning in the police station with that smug Detective Staves, answering questions about this poor friend of Charlie's who was found dead the other day. I suppose I shouldn't be hard on Staves, and perhaps I was just imagining it, but he seemed to be hiding things from both Charlie and me. And he seemed extremely suspicious. Even more so than before. I can't tell if it's me he doesn't trust, or my son."

This last comment once again forced Antigone to confront the utter blindness of Cornelius with regard to the possibility of his own guilt. But was that blindness willful, some sort of pose or protective cover? Intellectually, she felt less certain than ever of his innocence—there were too many coincidences and not enough explanations, no easy or even likely ways out of the labyrinth. And yet, at the same time, she also knew herself more emotionally committed to him than she had ever been to anyone in her life. And next to her stood the prototype, the only other person for whom she had felt anything like these depths of love and pity, her brother, Hiawatha.

More than Antigone herself, Hiawatha was strangely conscious that, along with everything else unfolding in this bedroom, a transfer was taking place in the affections of his sister. Suddenly, the events of the past few days, the family miseries that made up the web of their existences as similar nets trap or entangle the members of all families, were struck through and proved to be no more substantial than the cobwebs in the Vanderlyn cellar. What came to the foreground and seemed the only solid thing, the only tangible weapon with which to beat forward through the maze, was the loyalty that bound these otherwise isolated individuals together, Hiawatha (as always) to Antigone, Antigone (now and forever) to Cornelius, and Cornelius to . . . whom? To his missing son? For it was Charlie's disappearance that had brought him here tonight.

Cornelius had not interrupted his story while Hi and Tig were pondering these tangential topics. He had, in fact, continued quite breathlessly.

"First, Staves spoke to us separately. Then, before he said we might leave, he told us that he would definitely need to talk to us again, and that—it sounded so pompous at the time, and so unnecessary!—we shouldn't leave Westerly without his knowledge. So Charlie and I came home, had a terrible lunch together, during which he hardly spoke to me at all. Obviously he's out of his wits with grief. First his mother's body, then his best friend commits suicide! I told him I wanted him to stay with me until the police were finished with us. I told him I wanted to take him away for Christmas—to Italy, anywhere, but far away from here. He agreed without saying much. He said he was going to lie down. The next thing I knew, his bedroom was empty. He's not at the dorm. I called the campus police, and they said there was nothing they could do. After three or four hours, I became frantic, and thought I had better call Staves . . ."

At the mention of the name, there was a loud knock on the bedroom door, which opened before Professor Ross could reach it. There stood Laura Ross, her face and neck white above the burgundy edge of her dress, and with her, as though conjured out of the air, was Staves himself. He was not smiling, nor did he visibly register the presence of Hi and Tig. Instead he walked briskly to Cornelius. Behind him were two officers in uniform.

Staves spoke loudly and succinctly.

"Cornelius Vanderlyn, I am placing you under arrest for the murder of your wife, Virginia Scott Vanderlyn. Anything you say can and will be used against you . . ."

XXIII

IT WAS TWO O'CLOCK IN THE MORNING. HIAWATHA, in his old bathrobe, sat and sipped his hot chocolate and didn't even notice that the television was turned off. Beside him, his sister held, but completely forgot to drink, her Lapsang Souchong tea. Both remained quiet for long intervals before one of them, usually Antigone, would voice a speculation that they would ponder together for several more minutes till the other would reply.

"Well, it's clear they've found something."

Antigone was haunted by the harrowing image of Cornelius being taken away from the Ross house, his tragic, stunned face a cipher of blank disbelief against the busy chintz background of the canopy on the four-poster bed. But, ever logical, she kept her thoughts trained on the physical side of things. Clearly, Staves had discovered something.

After several moments of shared mind-racking, Hiawatha responded.

"Yes, but what on earth could it be?"

After another silent interim his sister spoke again.

"It must have something to do with that boy's death."

"But there's nothing we can do about it at this hour. And tomorrow I leave. I was thinking, as I change planes in New York, and there's a three-hour layover, maybe I could get in touch with that student, that designer, whom Virginia was said to have had an affair with. Didn't somebody say he lived in New York?"

"He wouldn't be much of a designer if he didn't live in New York," Tig declared without the usual pause. Her sour comment dismissing the cultural claims of all other American cities was partly a reflec-tion of her low spirits, partly of her distracted state of mind. It was beginning to look hopeless; at least it was true, as Hi had said, that there was nothing they could do tonight. But still, she couldn't conceive of going to bed, and Hi felt the same way. Suddenly a little flicker of interest animated her face.

"I'll tell you what," she said with rising energy. "Tomorrow morning, before you go back to Chicago—when does your plane leave?—we'll call that nice Professor Nolan's wife and ask her bluntly to tell us everything she knows. That way we don't have to talk to Staves again till we've done a little more investigating."

Antigone's spark was too fleeting to ignite Hiawatha.

"But Tig, my plane leaves at noon. And I have to say, though it sounds terribly old-fashioned of me," (but this made him secretly proud) "that I think you shouldn't do too much on your own. It may actually be dangerous, Tig, just like that gun-jumping, so-called detective Staves insists. He certainly gave us the snub this evening. Say, isn't 'dick' a synonym for 'detective'?"

Tig smiled wearily. "We'll have to ask Uncle Andrew." And then, more daringly, she added, "When you come home for Christmas."

Hiawatha was not quite up to his sister's attempt at humor. In fact, he reddened, before replying loftily, like one whose calm is forced and a clear warning that the opposite is on its way.

"I think it highly improbable, given the current state of things, that I will be spending this Christmas in Boston."

"Oh, Hi, I was joking! Don't be so crabby."

"I don't think you can say I'm being crabby, right after I'm kicked out of the house by dear old Dad." Hi was morosely defensive whenever this particular topic was raised.

Tig, in her own agitated state, absently responded with the truth, than which, in such situations, nothing is more provoking.

"But, Hi, he didn't kick you out. You left. As you always do."

"You heard the way he talks to me." Hi's eyes were wide at his sister's unwonted correction.

But before he could complete his retort, she interrupted him.

"Yes, you and Dad. Dad says nasty things and you run away. But you forget that with all your running off and being hurt, other people get hurt, too."

Antigone was uncharacteristically cross. If she had had more time to analyze the present circumstances, she would have seen that while she was speaking truthfully to her brother about their own family, she was thinking about the Vanderlyns. The anger in her voice stemmed from the frustration she felt at the arrest of Cornelius. But Hiawatha took her tone very personally, and stood up with a melodramatic sigh.

"Yes, I can only imagine how painful it must be for you and Mom to watch someone being mistreated.

Like the emperor's women at the gladiatorial games. Sorry to have upset you by being so pathetic."

And with this, Hiawatha stomped out of the room. Tig heard him clank his cup down in the kitchen sink, but she didn't rush off to appease him. Her thoughts were decidedly elsewhere. Still, a few minutes later, she got up to go to bed. The light was on in Hi's room. He was probably brooding, maybe pretending to read. She called through the door to him, but he didn't respond. She felt too tired to make things up immediately, though, getting ready for bed, she found herself tramping loudly around her room and back and forth to the bathroom, hoping that the noise would communicate to him her eagerness to at least say good-night. But he never responded, and she gave up when she saw the light beneath his door go off.

Hiawatha, for his part, lay furious under his covers, finally fed up with everybody. Including Tig. In his mind, he argued rationally, she had compounded their father's cruelty by accusing him of being insensitive and a coward. These were two things Hi was secretly terrified of being. So perhaps he was a coward. But insensitive? As an alternative to such irritating self-questioning, he turned his thoughts to the people he had met during the past week and a half in Westerly, all of whom, in his present mood, he positively loathed. With them, he found himself playing a rather

vengeful game that he had often used to occupy himself in bed as a child. He tried to picture each of his
new acquaintances as the animal he or she most obviously resembled, thereby transforming the recent mysterious events at Clare College into a kind of Beatrix
Potter tale. For example, with his bristling black hair
and his snorting manner, Chuck Vigevano was a boar,
one which, to judge from its temper, had gone a long
time without landing a truffle. Judy Wagner Dumont
was a gnat, plain and simple. And the overwhelming
Mrs. Hughes was a hybrid, a land whale with teeth.

And what was Cornelius? Again, it came back to
that.

And so, once again, despite their differences, both
brother and sister were preoccupied with the same
question when, at last, they fell asleep.

The next morning, there was little conversation
in the car as Tig drove her brother to the airport in
Albany. She had called Mrs. Nolan while Hi was
showering, and though the journalist had shown
herself eager to be of help, there was little she could
add to what her husband had told them at the Ross
party the previous evening. That Staves had somehow connected the young man's suicide—the police
were still referring to the death of Charlie's friend as
such—to the murder of Virginia Vanderlyn, was
beyond question. But as to the evidence they had

found, Mrs. Nolan could not speculate. She was able to tell Tig that the name on the dead boy's New York driver's license was, in fact, Matthew Smythson, and this Tig related to a taciturn Hiawatha, along with a summary of her telephone conversation, on their way to the airport. When they arrived, Hi jumped out of the car, grabbed his bag from the trunk, and, without looking her in the face, shook his sister's hand before hastening into the terminal. Apparently, he was still upset, and Antigone had an unhappy drive back to Westerly as the snow began to fall.

If Hiawatha had been upset on the way to Albany, he was livid when he arrived in New York to find his flight, and most other flights out of La Guardia, canceled because of the weather. The soonest he would be able to leave would be the next afternoon, unless, of course, the snow continued, in which case his departure would be postponed indefinitely. He groaned at the uniformed woman, who explained this to him from well behind her computer, and who nervously extended her hand in order to pass him his revised ticket and a three-dollar meal voucher. Hi walked away thinking that the entire airport looked like a trade hall hosting a convention of the dejected.

He himself was still feeling ashamed of the way he had fought with his sister. It was this, rather than ill

will—in fact, it was just the opposite of disaffection—
which had reduced him to silence this morning. Her
greater success, in and outside the family, often left Hi
feeling awkward and embarrassed. But he was prouder
of her than anyone else could be. And there she was,
probably thinking that he was just a big sulker.

Perhaps he could make it up to her. Since he had
to spend the night in New York—remaining at the airport for twenty-four hours was unthinkable—he
would get a hotel room, perhaps at the Roosevelt,
where he and Tig had stayed a number of times, and
make a few phone calls. He would track down Paul
Mullaney, the student who was said to be among Virginia's lovers. And then there was the mysterious
young friend of Charlie Vanderlyn, the so-called suicide, Matthew Smythson, whose driver's license
included an address near Columbia University. Surely
Hiawatha could uncover something to compensate his
sister for his bad behavior. Though she, too, he
reminded himself, had not been without blame.

Despite the blizzard, Hi felt almost lucky to have
an extra day to work on the mystery and looked forward to his night in New York.

XXIV

A T THE POLICE STATION, CORNELIUS HAD ACTUALLY spent the night in jail. It was strangely unhumiliating, and though not physically comfortable, he had borne up well. After all, as a graduate student, he had passed weeks in the desert in Jordan, with nothing approaching an amenity, sharing a single tent with six other men. It had been worth it to dig among the ruins of Petra. For that was all he had ever wanted to do—before Virginia and adulthood—to be an excavator. To bring things to light. Now, however, he had been accused of something quite the opposite of archeological. He had been accused, in fact, of brutally killing and burying his wife. The hypothesis was absurd enough to leave him outwardly cold, and even disinterested.

Inwardly, however, he was frantic with fear, and not for himself. What on earth had happened to Charlie? The question recurred to him at brief intervals in his distraction, like the violent twanging of a loose wire where his spinal cord should be. Even when Detective Staves, who was visibly losing patience with everybody connected to Clare College, suggested, after several hours of preliminary conversation, that he call his lawyer, Cornelius did so with only one goal in mind—that of tracking down his son. Of course, his cousin, Willem Vanderlyn III, Esq., had agreed to leave Boston immediately in order to accomplish Cornelius's release. He would no doubt arrive presently, but that seemed already too long to wait to locate the boy, who, for all anybody knew, might be in extreme danger. Staves had assured him that his son would be found, but Cornelius couldn't help thinking that this was a halfhearted, or perhaps even a menacing, promise.

Now, after a sleepless night in a jail cell, with his cousin on the way (the same cousin, in fact, who had once made such flagrant advances to Virginia), Cornelius was again brought in to be interrogated by a refreshed, but by no means refreshing, Detective Staves. The two men faced each other across the metal rectangle of the table, resembling chess players waiting for a board, or, more accurately, the sinner and the priest in a modern confessional, except it would have been difficult to say in the present circumstances which man was which. Staves, in particular, seemed to veer from one role to the other, his voice now coaxing and confidential, now pleading and even apologetic.

"I'm sorry to have to go through all this again, Professor Vanderlyn. But as you've agreed to talk to us before your lawyer arrives, I hope you won't mind . . ."

"Not at all, as long as you keep your promise that you're looking for Charlie."

Staves tried to smile knowingly in response to the professor's indication of paternal concern, but the smile felt false, and the effect was stupid. The fact was, the police chief didn't know what Vanderlyn was up to, hadn't yet figured him out, and so he was incapable of leading him where he wanted. Nevertheless, he continued to repeat the questions he had asked the night before.

"Did you or did you not kill your wife?"

Likewise, Cornelius repeated the same answers he had already given.

"No. Certainly not."

But inside, he was trying to remain calm, thinking to himself.

"*Life is a river.*" *Who said that?*

"Did you, or did you not, cancel the delivery of a new boiler system, scheduled to be installed at your old house—the house in which you were then living with your wife and child—on or about October 12, 1989, at the very time your wife disappeared?"

"I have no recollection at all of ever having done so."

Life is not only the river, but also the banks it runs between, and the invisible current that seems and is determined by other, larger forces—the wind, the earth, and, far above but never indifferent, the sky.

"Did you or did you not know Matthew Smythson, either by that name or by the name Michael Smith?"

"I've told you I knew him only as Michael Smith, and only as a friend of my son, Charlie."

The stream isn't merely the water, light and miraculous, but all the debris—the living things and the dead and the inanimate detritus it carries along.

"And you did not have any dealings with him before he was introduced to you by your son, or know before now that his real name was Matthew Smythson?"

"No."

Life doesn't merely move through us, but we are carried with it, and in us others are moved and abandoned and retrieved and again moved forward in time.

"Do you recognize this?"

Here was a break in the routine of interrogation established by the detective the previous evening. As such, it brought Cornelius back to the present time and place. He watched as Staves removed from his briefcase a small box and set it down on the table between them.

"No," said Cornelius, not without some curiosity.

"Open it," directed Staves.

Slowly, like a stag advancing out of the wild, Cornelius reached for the box. When he took it, he felt something like fear. The last time Staves had shown him something, it had been a relic of his dead wife's. And now, when he opened the box, history repeated itself.

He thought, at last, he might actually cry.

"Well?" pressed Staves.

"It's hers." Cornelius's voice was choked. Here was an artifact, at one time more precious to him than any other, that had, nevertheless, eluded him till now. The world, so much of which he had traveled and seen, contracted to the size of his palm and yet still seemed so much larger than everything else. He was shaking, but not afraid. At least, not for himself. Nor any longer, he realized sadly, for her.

Staves took the ring from Cornelius and continued with a mixture of pride and contempt.

"Look at the inscription, Professor Vanderlyn. 'Now and Forever, 10–10–80.' The day you were married, I believe? This is her wedding ring, isn't it? And you distinctly told me you hadn't seen it since your wife left. Odd, then, finding it where we did. On the smallest finger of the left hand of Matthew Smythson, the nineteen-year-old boy you say you hardly knew."

Cornelius wanted to speak. His natural intelligence told him that the ring hardly connected Cornelius to the murder of his wife, much less to that of the boy. But of course, Staves had never accused him of anything with regard to young Smythson, other than knowing him and seeing him the evening of his death. The dawning fear that the detective suspected Charlie of a crime as horrible as he himself was thought to have committed, filled the father with dread. If only he knew where Charlie was, or that he was safe, Cornelius would have confessed to everything. And then he thought of Antigone Musing. Perhaps she could find the boy . . .

But in the midst of these mute, desperate wanderings, there came a loud banging on the door of the room. Staves looked around furiously, like a cat cheated of its prey by an inferior interloper.

"What on earth!? Who is it?"

The door opened and in stomped an elegantly overcoated middle-aged man with whiskers, who looked like a picture of Martin Van Buren come to life. This was Cornelius's cousin, and when he entered the room, one glance at Staves made it clear that the interview was over.

XXV

WELL OUT OF SIGHT OF THE SPIRES OF CLARE, A young man was walking alone through the old cemetery across the road from the campus of St. Mark's preparatory school. To his right, the rising sun provided a glowing backdrop for the silhouette of the buildings he knew so well, including the dormitory where he had spent the previous night on the floor of his former roommate, Steve Lalonde. And to his left, the same sun flung out a little blanket of shade from each of the markers of the ancient dead. The young man felt, as he had never felt before, the ephemerality of his imprisonment and almost longed for it to end.

Leaving Westerly, leaving his father in his study and his mother in the morgue, leaving his dead friend there, too—he had been right to make so comprehensive an escape. But what had seemed to him clear and necessary only yesterday, turned out not to have been a solution to his problems, but only a deferment. His friend Steve had pointed this out, in his usual straightforward manner, immediately upon his arrival. The younger man was lying in bed in his mismatched pajamas with an ashtray balanced on his chest, while the older sat perpendicular to him at the end of the bed with his knees up, fully dressed.

"It certainly looks as though you've got a problem. I told you last year you should just dump your family and go hang out in Europe for awhile. Everybody who does that winds up having a very interesting life. You could become a hustler in Paris. Remember Mark Winfield, who graduated the year before you? Well, he did that, and it turns out he made more last year than his old man."

Steve Lalonde was not displaying any lack of feeling when he said this. A handsome seventeen-year-old with a round, perpetually-grinning face, he himself could claim vast firsthand experience with family problems. In fact, St. Mark's had never admitted a boy with a greater number of step-parents and half-siblings, and that was already three years ago. He pushed his glasses up on his face and tapped the ash from his cigarette, waiting for Charlie Vanderlyn to respond.

"But you don't know half of what's happened," said the latter at last, as though not entirely sure of how much to tell, or how much he *could* tell.

"Well, I've met your dad, and he definitely didn't do it. Teachers make believable victims, but highly implausible murderers. Except the ones who bore you to death."

Again, Charlie wasn't struck by any callousness in his friend's unfettered assessment of teachers in general, or the implications it might have for his father in particular. But as he had said, there was more to tell.

"Listen, Steve. Do you remember Matthew Smythson? He was a year ahead of me. Tall kid, not very athletic. Kind of a loner."

"Oh, yeah. I remember some guy you used to hang around with. A bit nutty, wasn't he? I thought maybe he made his own drugs or something. Not real friendly, as I recall. What about him?"

"Well, he's been hiding out from his own family in Westerly. I mean, not his family, since his mother's been dead for a couple of years, and his father . . . well, that's part of the story."

"Part of what story? The story about your mom?"

"No, I don't think the two stories are related. I mean, I don't see how they could be. But he came to

Westerly because he thought his father was someone who taught there. His mother was a professor at Columbia, a kind of free-love feminist type, and she never told him who his father was, and then after she died suddenly, he set out to find him. Something led him to Westerly, and I think he was onto someone. That's what he was doing there, until . . ."

"Until what?" said Steve, looking over the cigarette he was rolling.

"Until he died, too." Charlie gulped, but continued. "The police said it was suicide, but I was with him only hours before he was found, and . . ." He gulped again, as though to swallow and force down the knot of anguish rising in his throat.

"And what?" said Steve, sitting upright. He was becoming intrigued by his friend's tale.

"And I know it wasn't suicide. He was a bit depressed that night—it being Thanksgiving and all— but if anyone was suicidal, it was me. He was—how can I explain it?—kept alive by this search for his dad. It was like an obsession. Have you had Mr. Benson's Nineteenth-Century British Poetry class? Well, Matty was like Tennyson's Ulysses, living preternaturally for the quest."

Charlie blushed for the pedantry of his own allusion, as well as the way he had phrased it, which might have been interpreted by his friend as an omen of inherited academic inclinations. But Steve Lalonde was actually quite impressed, and remained silent. Charlie, who had already drunk most of the bottle of wine he had brought from his father's place, couldn't help sniffling a bit, and Steve remained appropriately respectful. At last, he offered Charlie a cigarette, and they smoked quietly together in the dark for some time, before going to sleep.

Now, with the sun coming up over Southborough, Charlie felt more lost than ever. He paused to examine some of the gravestones sprawling over the slope in front of the old white church, a sleeping congregation awaiting the unearthly wake-up call. "Here lieth the body of Elihu Geddes, aged seventeen yeares and four months." Would he, Elihu, be all that happy if he actually found himself back among the living? Charlie couldn't help but doubt it, though he was distracted from committing himself definitively on the subject by the loud yahooing of young Mr. Lalonde. The next moment, a football banged against the gravestone and landed in Elihu's lap. Charlie bent down, as though to pick it up, but then changed his mind and sat down on the cold grass instead, where Steve joined him.

"Charlie, take me out for breakfast. I can't deal with the dining hall today, and seeing as you've got a car ..."

Charlie looked up from the grave, then closed his eyes, all his features relaxed for a moment in the lambent flush of the new day. He felt a strange, fleeting sensation, an almost paternal but elusive tenderness for this high school student, who was, after all, only a year younger than himself. He thought of his own father back in Westerly, frantically looking for him (for if his father seemed hardly to notice him when he was around, he more than made up for it by the intensity of his searches when he was gone). He tugged at Steve's trouser leg to get his attention.

"I'll take you to breakfast if you answer one question."

"What is it?" said Steve, happy to go along.

"Is a thing true because you know it or because you feel it?"

"Well, I suppose that . . ."

"No! Don't answer right away," interrupted Charlie, rising up from the ground. "Think about it. We'll eat first. Then you can tell me."

And off they went.

XXVI

ANTIGONE MUSING STOMPED THE SNOW FROM HER shoes, more energetically than was absolutely required. The vigorous gesture was an expression of her mood; she was no happier to be inside her own front door than she had been walking home from the science building in the cold. The entire day, in fact, had been a series of disappointments, but disappointments of the sort that it is almost impossible to put aside, much less forget, with a simple change in the physical surroundings or the tipping of day toward night.

It was only four-thirty on Monday afternoon, and already it was dark. Tig simultaneously removed her shoes and her coat, and then switched on the light in her small front hallway. She headed automatically toward the kitchen to pour herself a glass of wine and to review her options for rescuing what remained of the waking day.

In the kitchen, she had the momentary illusion that Hiawatha was still with her, in the house, but then she reminded herself that he was, despite the terrible weather, undoubtedly back in Chicago by now. She was wishing he would call, but too proud as yet to do that herself, especially after his hasty getaway at the airport. And yet there were things she was dying to tell him.

She had spent the earlier part of the day preparing her eleven o'clock lecture; it was always a challenge, given the increasing restlessness of the students, to begin teaching again just after the Thanksgiving break, with a mere three weeks before the longer Christmas recess. Nevertheless, she had done her best, interrupting her work only to telephone Randall Ross in his office to find out if there was any news concerning Cornelius. There was none. As far as Ross could tell, Professor Vanderlyn was still in police custody, though, according to the newspapers, a family lawyer had come from Boston to negotiate at least a temporary release. Finally, just before going to class, Tig had actually telephoned Detective Staves, with the vague hope of speaking to Cornelius himself. Striving to communicate all the deference and humility she could muster, she made her request to the police chief, who replied curtly that Professor Vanderlyn was altogether inaccessible at the present time; then he added, in something more of his usual friendly manner, that he hoped she had had a nice holiday and he would be happy to keep her informed.

The way Antigone received this refusal of access to Cornelius did accomplish something. It made it clear to her, once and for all, that she was in love with him. And realizing this only intensified her frustration. Still, she entered the lecture hall with her characteristic poise and did a good job explaining the concept of resonance, a property due to which much of what we think of as solid, finite matter is actually open and, at the molecular level, disengaged. She was in the process of illustrating the point with the analogy of a cat's fur—the way it represents a living interface between the cat and its environment—when she happened to notice Charlie Vanderlyn's absence. Unsurprising in itself, this lacuna among her disciples made her pause in her explanation, and increased her inner sense of helpless dejection.

And then afterward, as she was eating lunch alone in her office, a relatively remarkable thing occurred. She received a telephone call from a Mr. Willem Vanderlyn, who identified himself as the

cousin of Cornelius, as well as his lawyer. He was
calling to communicate his cousin's continued grat-
itude for her help and kindness during the past
weeks and to determine whether or not she had
heard from Charlie Vanderlyn. She hastened to
inform him that the young man had, in fact, been
absent from class today, but that she would happily
do anything in her power to assist him or his father.
Mr. Vanderlyn acknowledged her generous offer,
but said that at the present time, he could only ask
that she inform him if Charlie should contact her.
The inactivity of waiting was not appealing to
Antigone, but she promised to keep in touch with
Cornelius's cousin, and hoped that he would do the
same for her. Then, with a final expression of grati-
tude on the part of Cornelius and himself, Mr. Vanderlyn hung up.

Now, sipping her wine in the window seat of her
warm cottage, Antigone considered the possibility of
actually going out to look for Charlie. Certainly he
was missing—that much had been clear from the
lawyer's call. But how on earth would she know
where to begin the search? She was staring into the
darkness of her little yard and beyond when a shadow
crossed the screen of her vision, quite close to the
house. She was startled, for it had seemed to be a
human form, but within seconds she was distracted

by the sound of her doorbell ringing. She rose quickly and, in an agitated state, opened her front door. She was surprised, but not unrelieved, to find that it was Randall Ross.

"Oh, it's you. Thank goodness," she started to say, but he cut her off immediately.

"Listen, Antigone, I'm sorry about dropping in like this. But I've got to talk to you."

Professor Ross seemed as agitated as Antigone herself. She wondered if their reasons were the same. As she was always happy to see this particular colleague, despite the unorthodoxy of his turning up without calling first, she welcomed him fervently into the house.

"Frankly, I'm very grateful for the company. I was scared when I saw someone behind the house," said Tig, taking Randall's coat. He didn't seem at first to hear her, so she continued. "But why have you come? Is it about Cornelius?"

"Well," Ross began, following his friend into her kitchen, "only tangentially, I think. It's got more to do with you. Thank you."

Ross took the glass of wine Tig held out for him, and they both walked into the living room, where they seated themselves on the sofa. Randall was apparently quite preoccupied with something. Finally, he turned and looked directly into her face.

"Antigone, I think I've been misleading you." He seemed to be groping for a way to begin what was not an easy speech.

How unlike the suave and charming Randall Ross to be at a loss for words, Tig had time to remark to herself, before he went on.

"I think, perhaps, I owe you an apology."

"Whatever for?" she wondered aloud.

"Well, to be honest, perhaps I have seemed to encourage your interest in Van—in Cornelius Vanderlyn. I can't help but notice your concern for him, and I've thought long and hard about the events of these last weeks—and these years, too, long before you came to Clare, when you were still a child . . ."

At this point, Ross paused and looked at Tig with a deep, but somehow thwarted, or at least in no way threatening, tenderness.

"And I think it may be dangerous, this involvement of yours."

Antigone was mystified. The attractions of Ross had never been lost on her, but she was not in love with him. And for all of Hiawatha's teasing, she had never seriously considered that he might be in love with her, either. Yet, here he was, an unanticipated guest, talking to her in the soft tones of a would-be protector, hoping to shield her from . . . what? She was further confused when, receiving no reply to his remarks, he put his wine glass down and, taking her hands in both of his, kissed them gently.

Flustered and embarrassed, Antigone pulled away.

"I'm sorry," whispered Ross, resting his elbows on his knees and his handsome head between his palms.

"You haven't done anything," Tig began, her own voice very low. "You're very kind to want to protect me. But I'm too confused to deal with such things right now. It isn't only Cornelius's arrest. It's everything. Hi and I had a fight, and he hardly said goodbye. Charlie Vanderlyn seems to have disappeared. And that poor friend of his, Matthew Smythson—I can't help thinking about his death, and that it's somehow a clue to everything else."

At the moment in this litany when Antigone spoke the name of Matthew Smythson, Randall Ross, who had been listening without concentrating, sat up straight.

"Smythson? Was that the boy's name?"

"Yes. He was from New York, apparently. Not a student at all. But you knew that already from your colleague, Mr. Nolan."

"But I didn't know his name. It wasn't in the newspapers, that I saw."

"Do you know him?" Tig thought it was rather curious, this sudden change in Ross's posture and tone. And it was even more curious when, after answering almost inaudibly in the negative, he rose abruptly and said that he thought he had better go. Tig followed him in some bewilderment to the front hall, where he swiftly slipped into his coat, and then, pausing before the open door, kissed her on the cheek. His last words to her, uttered with emotion but also in haste, were "Take care, Antigone, my dear," and then he was swallowed up in the snowy darkness.

Tig, feeling that Ross's bizarre visit was a perfectly fitting ending to a most enigmatic and irritating day, headed straight into her bedroom, where she intended to change into her pajamas, thereby expressing sartorially her resolve not to leave the house again, but to have an early dinner and then to get some sleep. In her room, she stood before the dressing table where she kept her telephone answering machine and played back the one message she had received. It was Hiawatha's voice, all frantic and out of focus.

"Hello, Tig, it's Hi. I'm calling from New York, where I've been snowed in . . ."

But here the message was interrupted, as all of a sudden, the electricity in the house went off with a loud crack. Tig found herself in the dark, groping her way around the bed in order to retrieve a flashlight from her dresser drawer. This was not the first power outage she had been forced to deal with, and while this one might have been caused by the weather, it was also possible, given the age of the house, that it was merely the fuse. Her fuse box was in the basement, and so, finding the flashlight, she made her way in that direction.

At the top of the stairs leading down from the kitchen, something made her pause. It was as though, in the darkness below, that same indistinct but undoubtedly human form she had seen earlier outside the house, had now reappeared inside it. And yet, it moved too swiftly, too knowingly, among the shadows to be real. A scientist through and through, Antigone overcame the instinct to be afraid. She remembered with a smile the bat that had frightened her and Hi at the Vanderlyn house.

On one of the middle stairs, she heard a slight scratching noise. It actually sounded far away. The darkness, which seemed exaggerated by the single beam of light with which she bored through it, was playing tricks on her ability to perceive distances. Perhaps an animal had taken shelter from the weather in her basement. No doubt that was it. Still, she couldn't help but register, for the briefest second, an instinctive sense of relief that the floor of her basement was concrete and could not be utilized for the discarding of human corpses.

She stopped. There it was again. Closer this time, she thought.

She found herself recalling the pompous Italian at the Rosses' party, who claimed to have heard a scratching noise at that house the night the Smythson boy was murdered.

For Antigone knew, somehow, that he had been murdered.

She took the last two steps, stopped, and then spun round again when she heard a violent crash upstairs. It sounded as though her front door had exploded. And when she turned around, she was instantly brought down by a severe blow to the back of her head. She was conscious of nothing else—not the scuttling of numerous feet, nor the loud human cry, followed moments later by another in a somewhat lower register.

The next thing she knew, she was lying in the back of an ambulance, with a terrible ache running from her head all the way down her spine. And a man was sitting next to her, staring down at her, squeezing her hand, but otherwise perfectly still. It was her brother, Hiawatha, and he was crying, as it seemed from his face, for terror and joy.

XXVII

Y OU LOOK LIKE JOAN OF ARC!" DECLARED HI, WHO
had been piping up with such comparisons at
brief, irregular intervals for almost an hour. She had
already been told that she resembled a tennis ball, a
plucked chicken, a victim of the first world war and a
variety of cinematic artists, from Jean Seberg to Erich
von Stroheim.

"Joan of Arc?" queried Mr. Staves.

"You know. Right before she's burned."

"Make up your mind," responded Tig. She was
seated on the sofa in her own living room, in a volu-
minous bathrobe, with her legs up, flanked by the two
men. Sure enough, her hair had been shorn off at the

hospital, where she had spent the previous night, after the attack. She had needed numerous stitches, and they had cut all of her hair to better assess the extent of the damage. Now she had a large white bandage covering much of the back of her skull, which was otherwise quite bare. It would not have been particularly surprising to anyone who knew her that the razor had not diminished her prettiness in the slightest. Or, as Hi had said, not by a hair.

"I'm still waiting for the full explanation," Antigone intoned again, after a pause to take a sip of the tea that her brother was holding for her. "I simply can't believe that Randall Ross was involved."

Both her brother and the detective began to speak, but Hi, who was feeling unusually buoyant and heroic after the part he had played in his sister's rescue, politely deferred to the policeman. He leaned back further into the cushions at the end of the couch, ready to interrupt the detective's story if the need arose. On the other side of Antigone, Staves assumed a pose which reminded her of that adopted by Professor Ross only hours earlier in the same room: elbows on knees and head between hands.

"Well, he probably wasn't involved in the original crime, except unknowingly. And last night, according to his own testimony, which I tend to believe, he really was motivated to see you by a sense of concern, a feeling that you were in danger."

"He was so odd," said Tig, eating one of the chocolates Detective Staves had brought, before handing them to Hi.

"He was probably beginning to piece things together," the detective continued. "Though, from his formal statement this morning, he had no notion at all that there was a connection between the events of ten years ago and the murder of Matthew Smythson."

"And what a connection!" exclaimed Tig, still rather dazed.

"It's thanks to your brother that we know that," Staves happily conceded.

Hi beamed at the recognition, then proceeded to retell his tale.

"Yes, as I told you in my message, which was cut off when she cut the power, I was stuck in New York, and I felt like I'd let you down when I left." He didn't, surprisingly, pause to make a sheepish face when he said this, as Tig expected he would. "So, since I had a little time, I called Paul Mullaney from the hotel. He's the guy who was said to have slept with Virginia when he was still an undergraduate at Clare. As soon as he realized that I was not working with the police," here he glanced playfully at Staves, "and that I was

not trying to dig up dirt on Virginia which might
make it seem like she deserved what she got, he was
very interested in talking to me. To say the least. He
actually came to the hotel, and explained that, first of
all, he had never been Virginia's lover. That he had
been gay since the third grade." Hi paused to ask tangentially, "Is that possible? I mean, could you be gay
in the third grade?"

"I couldn't," said Staves. His tone marked the
void between his own generation and that of his
companions.

"Anyway, he did love Virginia and thought it was
hysterically funny that he was rumored to be the
object of her immoral advances. But beyond talking
about Virginia's character, he wasn't much help. He
did say, however, that he thought she had had an
affair with Randall Ross, though she had never come
right out and acknowledged it. But she had once let
slip that she had known him before she was married."

Here Staves felt obliged to interject some information of his own.

"Yes, it turns out that Virginia actually worked in
a secretarial pool in Cambridge as a young woman. It
was there, we know, that she met Cornelius Vanderlyn,
when he was on a month-long fellowship at Harvard.
She had always been popular with brainy people—the
Marilyn Monroe-Arthur Miller syndrome. What we

never considered particularly significant was the fact that Randall Ross was also a visiting fellow at Harvard that year, in the English Department. He has now confessed that he knew her there, and that, practically speaking, he followed her to Clare after her marriage."

"But why wasn't Ross ever suspected?" Tig couldn't help but wonder aloud. "After all, she was accused of having slept with almost everyone she met." Tig recalled considering the possibility of a liaison between Ross and Virginia, and then dismissing it.

"Yes, wherever it began—whether here or in Boston—Mrs. Vanderlyn kept that particular relationship to herself. It was her only secret, and it cost her her life. She didn't even tell her best friend, Hermione Pole, though I think Miss Pole suspected it. And can you guess why she guarded it so carefully and so well?"

Tig could not guess, so her brother helped her out.

"What was the one thing everybody agrees that she cared about in her life?"

It dawned on Tig, but the realization did not make her happy.

"Her son, Charlie. Of course! He's really Ross's son."

Hi hardly noticed the faint groan that seemed to accompany his sister's declaration. The deduction, clearly, made her unhappier than ever for Cornelius.

And where was he now? she was dying to ask. But she patiently allowed the two men to continue their tale.

"We won't know without a blood test, and that isn't necessarily in the cards," said Staves. "But it does seem likely."

"And Laura must have found out. And that's why she killed her."

"Exactly," said Staves and Hi, stereophonically.

"But why, 'exactly'? And how?" Like most tragedies, this one was at once simple and difficult to understand.

"Laura Ross, for all her apparent indifference to the world, for all her cool grace and quiet manners, is a regular volcano," explained the police chief with obvious relish. Here was a passionate criminal maniac that he could sink his bloodhound teeth into. "She had fallen in love with Ross when she was still a student at Wellesley, where Ross had done his first teaching. She left school to marry him. She wanted very badly to have children, but they never succeeded. She knew of his philandering and grew obsessed with her rivals. The most hated of all of these, for countless reasons, was Virginia Vanderlyn. Outwardly, she became a defender of Virginia in the college community. But all the while, she was keeping an eye on her, waiting to strike. She might even have guessed that Charlie was her husband's son. She might even have thought that the three of them were going to leave together. So she killed her and buried her and that was the end of that. Till now, when she found she had to kill again. First Matthew Smythson. Then you."

"I knew Matthew Smythson was murdered," said Tig. "But I can't, for the life of me, see a connection."

"Back to me!" Hi interjected. "As I was saying earlier, Paul Mullaney wasn't a great help with regard to Virginia's murder. But when I explained about the Smythson boy's death, and that I was going to look into that, too, he was eager to help out. So we went together to the Upper West Side address that was on the kid's driver's license. Of course, it was an apartment, and nobody was home, but we knocked on the neighbor's door, and a very friendly, middle-aged man—clearly not a New Yorker by birth—explained to us that people by the name of Smythson had lived there, a woman and her son. There had never, as far as he knew, been a father. The mother, a good-looking woman—something of a hippie type, he said, but very nice when you got to know her—had been a professor at Columbia. She had died in an accident while the son was in his senior year at St. Mark's School in Southborough. He hadn't seen the boy in at least a year, though he was sure there must have been a little money there.

"Anyway, Paul and I walked straight to Columbia, where we tracked down the specific department in which Ms. Smythson worked, a sort of sub-department, actually, called the Institute for Gender-Related Cultural and Sociological Proclivities, which sounded to me like a treatment center for unmentionable diseases. But the people there turned out to be both clean and normal. They knew about Matthew, but none of the administrative staff had seen him in ages. The head secretary brought me a sort of brochure—it was more like a yearbook, actually—which she thought might be of interest. She was right. The booklet had been produced to honor the late Professor Smythson, who had, it turned out, begun her career as a scholar of English literature. And there, among the many pictures of Ms. Smythson in action—in the classroom, on committees, that sort of thing—was a photograph taken in 1978, of her as chairperson of an international conference on eighteenth-century poetry. And can you guess who was sitting beside her in the photo, who was the co-chair of the event, and who turned up next to her in at least two of the other photographs?"

Yes, Tig could guess.

"Randall Ross. And I'll bet he looked the same twenty years ago as he does today. So what did you do?"

"I immediately called Staves. I mean, Mr. Staves. The famous detective." Hi could not help smiling, because his sister was still alive. "You see, it fit in perfectly with this strange feeling I had the night they

arrested Cornelius. You know how, when you're buy-
ing a shirt, sometimes you can't tell if a certain color
is black or very dark blue. What do you do?"

Tig and the detective exchanged glances. Hi had
almost lost them. But he went on.

"You find something that you know to be black,
and you compare the two. Well, the night the police
came to take Cornelius away, I felt distinctly that he
wasn't the murderer. I felt it, because the real murderer was in the room, too. Do you see?"

"But you thought it was Randall Ross. And it turned
out to be Laura," objected Tig, and Staves smiled.
"And I still don't understand why she killed Matthew
Smythson, even if it turned out that he, too . . ." Here
she wanted to groan again, remembering how Ross
had outlined his generation's attitude toward sexual
freedom with an authority that was certainly being
confirmed now. " . . . was Professor Ross's son."

"Well, Laura Ross was in the room, too," Hi
reminded his sister, a bit defensively.

At this point Staves took up the narrative.

"Your brother made the connection between
Ross and Smythson, and that was important. But he
couldn't have known about Laura's direct involvement. When he called me, I realized that Smythson
was the pivotal figure in the case. We already knew
that he was somehow linked to the Vanderlyn murder,

because he had been found with Virginia's wedding band on his finger. Now that made no sense. Luckily for us, Charlie Vanderlyn came back yesterday afternoon to add everything he knew. The kid was pretty shaken up when he found out his father was in jail, but that only made him more cooperative. He told us all about Matthew's being in Westerly incognito, as you might say, trying to find his father. And he said that he had actually helped Matthew to break into Hever Hall one night, though once they had gotten in, Matthew had laughed the escapade off as a joke and suggested they go home.

"Everything I tell you now is circumstantial, if not downright conjecture, but I think that Smythson probably returned to Hever Hall later the same night that he and Charlie broke in. I think he knew that Ross was his father, and he went looking for some sort of evidence in his office. Ross has finally admitted that he had some letters of Virginia's, from before she was married that, for obvious reasons, he preferred not to store at home, though he couldn't bring himself to throw them away. You poetry types are all the same."

"Don't look at me!" cried Tig. "Go on."

"And most vital of all, he kept her ring there. You see, he had seen Virginia the day she disappeared. He had fought with her and tried to talk her out of leaving.

According to him, he had absently picked up the ring from her dressing table and pocketed it. He really is a very sentimental guy. Or maybe he was trying, in his own tiny way, to protect his friend, Cornelius, from the finality of the blow that the abandoned wedding ring would have symbolized. In any case, Smythson got hold of it. Perhaps he assumed that the ring had belonged to his mother. After all, the date was about right. The poor kid had no idea how quickly academics change beds."

"If only," said Hi, like an actor in a play. He had never been more lighthearted in his life.

"Anyway," Staves seemed just about to conclude his story, "at some point Laura Ross must have found out about Smythson's investigation. She probably had no idea who he was at first, but she had a lot more to hide than her husband, and she was determined to protect them both. Remember, the body of Virginia Vanderlyn had just been discovered, and that probably made her a bit nervous. And while I mention it, it's more than likely that she herself canceled the installation of the boiler just after committing the crime. Having secretly followed her husband to Virginia's house on the day of the murder, which she had probably done on numerous occasions prior to that, and having listened to their fight from the cellar where she was hiding—remember, she was a frequent guest there, and knew the house quite well—she realized her good luck in at last finding Virginia on the verge of departure. There was even a good-bye note. But that kind of departure wasn't good enough for Laura. After she'd killed the woman, she probably called to cancel the boiler because she didn't want anyone to find the body, at least not right away, however unlikely it was that it would be connected to her. Even Mr. Vigevano can't say who precisely it was who made or took the call.

"So, back to last week. As far as we can surmise, she made a plan to meet Matthew Smythson behind her house on the night of Thanksgiving. She probably promised him some information, perhaps in exchange for something incriminating he had found, and then, when he showed up, she would just kill him. She was strong and fast, as you, Miss Musing, can testify. Her husband would be sound asleep in their bedroom at the front of the house, and, after all, the ground was still soft. But then, at the last minute, she found out that her husband had invited their Italian friend to stay, and the only guest bedroom was at the rear of the house. The Italian heard a noise that night. It was probably Matthew, trying to get Mrs. Ross's attention. She presumably came down, told him to meet her later at the clock tower, and there, she killed him. That it was premeditated is clear from the fact that she struck him with a small but heavy concrete plug;

it was this fact that led to the initial misreport that he had either fallen or jumped to the concrete paving. Though disguising the manner of his death was hardly a priority."

"So it was the method of her killing that remains the constant throughout all these crimes," said Tig, touching very gently the bandage on her head. "And what made you come to rescue me when you did?"

"That was your brother, of course. When he learned what he did in New York, he called me, and though I wasn't immediately available, he left a message. Then he took a train to Albany and came directly to the station. You must have been on your way home. In any case, he convinced me that something was up, and we tried calling you again, but the phone was busy. As we got close to your place, and saw that yours was the only dark house on the street, we became a bit concerned. Busy phone, black house. So at Hi's insistence—but without his actual physical input, I must say—my sergeant and I broke the door down. And though, of course, I'm sorry that you had to take such a blow, it did allow us to catch Mrs. Ross in the act."

"Oh, Tig, you should have seen her!" Hi burst in. "Terrifying! Trapped like a rat, flailing and hissing and screaming, as though with the accumulated wrath of all scorned women since the beginning of time. And then, as Detective Staves will tell you, not a word since her arrest. As though she were finally empty, entirely spent."

Hiawatha's vivid description of the capture of Laura Ross silenced them all. Tig suddenly felt exhausted; perhaps her pills were wearing off. Her limbs felt heavy. Staves recognized the change in her tone, and got up to leave.

"Of course, we never will know the extent of Randall Ross's collusion. His wife's silence could be interpreted as a way of protecting him. Contrary to what you might gather from television, we hardly ever find out what really happened at the actual scene of a crime." Then changing the subject, he added insightfully, "Cornelius has been released. I half expected to see him here."

No one responded.

Then Hiawatha rose, too.

"Mom should be here within the hour. She sounded so glad to have an excuse to come to visit. And very proud of you, surviving and all."

"And Dad?" Antigone wondered.

Hiawatha studied his sister's face in order to determine if she were being facetious again. She was perfectly inscrutable, so he gave her the benefit of the doubt.

"I didn't talk to him. When he answered the phone, I disguised my voice, and told him I was calling from the Salvation Army about a pickup, and could I please speak to Mrs. Musing about her battered lowboy."

Now it was Tig who studied her brother's face, which was equally inscrutable.

"Will I see you at Christmas?" she began, struggling to her feet to accompany them to the door. Surprising as it may have seemed, Staves had offered to drive Hiawatha to the airport in Albany; he was now several days late for work.

"In your dreams, I hope, sister dear."

Tig walked slowly behind Hiawatha to the door. She felt great waves of sadness, her limbs seemed pulled down by them as by the motions of the sea. So they were brothers, she thought, Charlie Vanderlyn and Matthew Smythson. Though they didn't even know it. And somehow, the saddest thing about that—even sadder than the horrible death of the one and the tragic life of the other—was that both of them had gone for years in ignorance, as though they were the ones who had been buried, buried almost at birth, living underground, uncertain of being loved, too young and too afraid ever to put the question too bluntly. There was the mystery, she thought, the mute, inexplicable loneliness of people, compared to which the brutal or irresponsible acts of Randall or Laura Ross were crisply defined and animalistic—no less ugly, but of no extraordinary interest.

Antigone thought of her own loneliness, too, from which all her knowledge and the energetic range of her interests were inadequate to distract her. And for the first time since it had happened, she registered the traumatic experience of the night before, and her own near-death. If she had been brought down, once and for all, would it have been as though she had never existed? If she had been buried alive, would Cornelius, the loneliest one of all, have understood, and descended, Orpheus-like, into that other world to find her?

Antigone and Hiawatha set a precedent by hugging in the hall. She waved good-bye to her brother and Detective Staves.

They drove off. It was really over.

Despite the cold air, she continued to lean against the open door.

He was coming up the walk, carrying a great bunch of yellow flowers.

EPILOGUE

J UNE, THEN."
Antigone Musing was sitting in the dining room of her parents' home. It was Christmas Eve, and the table was lavishly set, though it was long before dinnertime. Next to her sat Cornelius Vanderlyn, who had come from Westerly to spend the holiday with her. Otherwise, they were alone. Mrs. Musing had cleverly arranged that her husband should be out making a last-minute purchase of wine when Professor Vanderlyn arrived. She herself was not at all clear as to how she felt about the probability of her brightest daughter becoming engaged to a man old enough to be her father. And a man with such a history! But she knew

that, whatever the outcome, her own energies would be best directed toward giving them both some room.

Cornelius Vanderlyn was, to say the least, sensitive to his position with regard to Antigone and her family. He deplored playing the suitor, and this was not so much due to his age as to his temperament, or what had become of it. He couldn't help but feel that he had already had his chance at life, and it had been a failure. The result of such doubts, however, rendered him, ironically, almost boyishly shy. But it was already too late to doubt that she loved him or that he could think of living without her.

It will not, I hope, surprise the reader to learn that it was Cornelius's son, Charlie, who had helped his father to find the courage to seek out Antigone and even to pursue her, if that is the proper term. In long twilight discussions among the old pots and pictures in his father's dusty sanctuary, the young man had taken great pains and employed an extraordinary range of analogical arguments (which, Cornelius couldn't help but speculate, boded well for a scholastic future), to prove that his old man was still entitled to happiness. He had finally gained his point by reminding his father that Judy Wagner Dumont would never rest while Cornelius was single. A strange new intimacy grew up between the two men. And Charlie Vanderlyn would always be Charlie Vanderlyn.

Charlie had left this morning for Europe for the holidays with one of his high school friends, a deliberate act intended to encourage his father's freedom. The latter was studying Antigone Musing's profile against the bright squares of glass that made up the long vertical window behind her. Her hair was growing back; today she looked less like Joan of Arc than the figure of Athena in the metope of the Stymphalian birds from the temple of Zeus at Olympia, all quiet interest and infinite humanity. That was what she had come to personify for him, the irrefutable truth that the gods, when they are good, resemble the best of us.

Antigone, for her part, was thinking of her happiness, approaching it like some new element that would force her to revise the periodic charts of her past. She had wanted Cornelius from the moment she had met him; nothing else mattered. He had breathed innocence into her open but unbelieving heart. She could touch him when he wasn't there, even, or especially, among the beakers and lenses of her teaching laboratory.

"June, then," she repeated, turning to him. It would all be very old-fashioned. Hiawatha would approve.

At the thought of her brother, Antigone felt a pang. She had never missed him more than during these past few days, for he alone would be able to understand and, in so doing, increase her unbounded joy. And if he were there, he would see for himself that he could never be replaced in her affections. He would always be a living part of whoever she was.

Cornelius smiled palely. After a long silence—for theirs had been, from the start, an almost tacit affair—he asked, with equal parts humor and earnestness, "Is ours a tragedy or a love story?"

Antigone stared up into his face. It was true; he was a handsome and distinguished middle-aged scholar. But he was also a youthful, inconceivably beautiful blend of creature and soul, and there were moments when she tended to doubt his reality. She embraced him now with some force. Then, with more wisdom than either of them knew, but with a solemn and unquestioning resignation worthy of her classical namesake, she replied, "Oh, my dear. There is no difference, as you know."

Outside, Hiawatha alighted from the taxi and paid the driver. He stood for a moment, looking at the lights of the Christmas tree twinkling in the window at the front of the only home he knew.

"Well, you can't beat them until you join them," he murmured to himself.

Then he rubbed his ungloved hands together, grabbed his grandfather's suitcase, and sprang ambiguously up the steps to the door.